THE BIG SURPRISE

Melanie raced to the window and peered out to the driveway where a gigantic blue and silver custom van stood glinting in the late afternoon sun. Her friends ran to join her, gaping.

"It's gorgeous!" Melanie shrieked. "And it will hold a ton of kids. Dad, did you get a raise?"

Mr. Edwards shook his head. "This is all your mother's doing. Tell them about it, dear."

"Well, you know how long we've talked about going camping in the summer and even making ski trips in the winter. Your dad and I have looked at vans lots of times thinking that they would be ideal, but they are so expensive that we knew we couldn't buy one. Then I got the idea of using it to start a new business," she said. Her eyes were glowing with pride.

Melanie looked curiously at her mother. She had a funny feeling in the pit of her stomach. "What kind of business?"

"A teen taxi service," her mother said proudly. "I'm going to drive kids back and forth to Wakeman Junior High."

Melanie exchanged horrified looks with her friends. A taxi driver for kids at Wacko Junior High? Her own mother? She would be so embarrassed that she'd die!

THE FABULOUS FIVE

Teen Taxi

BETSY HAYNES

A BANTAM SKYLARK BOOK®

NEW YORK · TORONTO · LONDON · SYDNEY · AUCKLAND

RL 5, IL age 009–012

TEEN TAXI
A Bantam Skylark Book / May 1990

Bantam Books are published by Bantam Books, a division of Bantam Doubleday Dell Publishing Group, Inc. Its trademark, consisting of the words "Bantam Books" and the portrayal of a rooster, is Registered in U.S. Patent and Trademark Office and in other countries. Marca Registrada. Bantam Books, 666 Fifth Avenue, New York, New York 10103.

PRINTED IN THE UNITED STATES OF AMERICA

OPM   0 9 8 7 6 5 4 3 2 1

Teen Taxi

CHAPTER

1

"Where's little Beth?" Beth Barry asked anxiously. "I don't see her."

"Here she is," said Jana Morgan, reaching into the large cardboard box at the bottom of the basement stairs and pulling out a wiggly brown puppy, which she handed to Beth. "She was underneath Katie."

Katie Shannon grinned and held up another tiny dog whose curly red hair was amazingly close to the color of hers as Jana picked up her own brown and white namesake and snuggled it lovingly on her shoulder.

"Shhh!" cautioned Melanie Edwards. "Don't let my mom hear you calling them by their names. That's a secret. Remember?"

1

Melanie scooped up Scott, Shane, and Garrett, three of the four males in the litter of eight puppies Rainbow had given birth to shortly after the Edwardses had rescued her from the animal shelter at Christmastime. She headed up the basement stairs with the mother dog at her heels. The rest of The Fabulous Five had come home with Melanie after school, as they did once or twice a week, to help her take the puppies into the backyard for their afternoon play and exercise time.

When the five friends had closed the back door behind themselves and were sitting cross-legged in a circle in the grass with the puppies scampering around them, Melanie went on.

"I really don't understand my parents at all. They say I'll get extra attached to the puppies if I name them, which I did secretly anyway. They also say that we're going to have to start finding homes for them since they're getting so big." Melanie paused a moment and shrugged. "But sometimes, from the way they act, I wonder if they're planning to keep all eight puppies *plus* Rainbow."

Christie Winchell looked up from where the yellow puppy who had her name was nibbling on her finger. "Why do you say that?"

"For one thing, the pups have been weaned for ages," Melanie explained, "but Mom and Dad don't ever do anything about giving them away. And I'm pretty sure they sneak down to the basement and play with them when Jeffy and I aren't looking. Not that I'm complaining," she added with a laugh. "I want to keep them all."

"Well, you know how parents are," Beth assured her. "Totally unpredictable."

"You can say that again," said Melanie, rolling her eyes toward the sky.

"Personally, I think it's super that you named the four girl puppies after your four best friends," said Katie. "And nobody is surprised that you named three of the boys Scott, Shane, and Garrett, but what did you finally decide to name the fourth boy?"

Melanie blushed, knowing her friends thought she was totally boy crazy. And it was true that she had not had any trouble naming Scott, Shane, and Garrett after the three boys she had major crushes on, but deciding what to call the fourth one had not been so easy. There were tons of cute boys at Wakeman Junior High, like Derek Travelstead and Tim Riggs, but nobody else who she thought was really special.

"I know. You named him Brian, after Brian Olsen," teased Beth. "Hi, little Brian. *Sweet* little Brian," she cooed, holding up a roly-poly white puppy so that its nose touched hers. His little tail began wagging furiously, and his tiny pink tongue lapped at her nose.

"Poor dog!" cried Jana, falling backward into the grass and bursting out laughing. "Not Brian Olsen. Give me a break!"

"Seriously, though, I saw Brian Olsen looking at you in the cafeteria today, Mel," said Christie.

"Drooling, you mean," said Katie dryly.

"Oh, guys," Melanie groaned. "What am I going to do about him? I mean, you *know* how he is."

Her friends nodded sympathetically, and she had a pretty good idea what they were thinking. Brian Olsen was the last boy on earth she could ever have a crush on. He was the biggest boy in school and a total show-off. He was so proud of his muscles that he used to sneak up on unsuspecting girls and lift them over his head. The school principal, Mr. Bell, had put a stop to that, but he hadn't been able to do anything about Brian's obnoxious personality. And now, as horrible as it was, Brian had a crush on Melanie.

"I don't know," said Jana, shaking her head. "I hate to say this, but I'm glad it's you he likes and not me. That boy doesn't know when to take no for an answer."

"You've got my sympathy, too," said Beth, and the others nodded.

"So what did you name the fourth boy?" asked Christie. "We all know it wasn't Brian."

Melanie grinned sheepishly. "You're going to

laugh when I tell you," she said. "I named him Jason after Jason Rider, the actor who plays Chad in the soap opera *Interns and Lovers*. Ever since I bought Jason's life-size poster at the celebrity auction and hung it in my room where I can see it every day, I've decided that he's the most handsome guy alive."

"You're *kidding*!" Katie groaned, just as Melanie had known she would.

"I don't believe it either," said Beth. "Do you mean to say you think he's more handsome than Scott?"

"More handsome than Shane?" demanded Christie.

"Or Garrett?" chimed in Beth.

Melanie could tell her friends were all trying hard not to lose it and break into giggling fits. "Just be glad I didn't name him after any of your boyfriends," she said slyly. "I mean, I could have called him Randy or . . . hmm, let's see, Keith or—"

"Melanie! You and the girls come here. I've got something wonderful to show you!"

Mrs. Edwards had just come out the back door and was motioning excitedly. Exchanging shrugs with her friends, Melanie scrambled to her feet and looked to see that the gate was closed so that the puppies couldn't get out of the backyard. "Come on, guys," she said. "Let's go see what the big surprise is all about."

She led her friends into the kitchen where her father was absolutely beaming. Next to Mr. Edwards stood her little brother, Jeffy, his eyes dancing, and he held both hands over his mouth as if trying to keep words from escaping. "I won't tell her!" he burst through open fingers an instant later. "I promise not to tell!"

Melanie's heart leapt. "Come on. *Somebody* tell me," she insisted. "What's going on?"

"Go ahead, Mom," her father said. "You tell her. You're the one who's making it all happen."

"Okay," said Mrs. Edwards. She took a deep breath and Melanie could see that her mother was tingling with excitement. "You know how long we've needed a new car. Our old station wagon spends more time in the repair shop than in our garage."

Her mother paused again, and Melanie bounced on her toes in anticipation. "Do you mean, we got a new car? Is that what you're trying to say?"

"It's a van! It's a van!" shouted Jeffy. "A BI-I-G-G one!"

Melanie raced to the window and peered out to the driveway where a gigantic blue and silver custom van stood glinting in the late-afternoon sunlight. It *was* big and probably the most beautiful van she had ever seen. Her friends ran to join her, gaping.

"It's gorgeous!" she shrieked. "And it will hold a ton of kids. Dad, did you get a raise?"

Mr. Edwards shook his head. "This is all your mother's doing. Tell them about it, dear."

"Well, you know how long we've talked about going camping in the summer and even making ski trips in the winter. But you also know that our old station wagon was not dependable anymore, not to mention being too small for those kinds of trips. Your dad and I have looked at vans lots of times, thinking that they would be ideal, but they are so expensive that we knew we couldn't buy one. Then I got the idea of using it to start a new business," she said. Her eyes were glowing with pride. "The money I make will more than make the payments, and we'll be able to do all the things we've always wanted to do."

Melanie looked curiously at her mother. She had a funny feeling in the pit of her stomach. "What kind of business?" she asked.

"A teen taxi service," her mother said proudly. "I'm going to drive kids back and forth to Wakeman Junior High."

Melanie heard someone groan and knew it must be herself. "You're *what*?"

"That's right, sweetheart. I've got it all worked out on paper. There are plenty of kids whose parents work and can't drive them to school but who also live too close to school to be on a bus route. They need transportation, and I'm going to provide it with the new van. I'm even having a sign made for the side of the van. It's going to say EDWARDS'S TEEN TAXI. Isn't it exciting?"

Melanie exchanged horrified looks with her friends. *But Mom!* she tried to say, but even though she formed the words with her lips, no sound came out. She felt as if she were shrinking, and her whole life passed in front of her eyes in a blinding flash. A taxi driver for kids at Wacko Junior High? Her own mother? She would be so embarrassed that she'd die!

CHAPTER

2

"I can't believe your mom is really serious about running a taxi service for kids at Wacko," said Beth when Melanie met her friends at their regular spot by the school fence the next morning.

Melanie nodded. "Oh, brother. Is she ever serious. She says that the school district changed the bus routes this year to cut expenses, and now they include only kids who live more than two miles from school instead of one mile, the way it used to be. She says now lots of kids whose parents work are stranded with no way to get to and from school."

"That's true," said Katie. "Or else they have to come really early, before the school is open, so they can catch a ride with their parents. Shawnie Pendergast's mother drops her off on the way to her job. She says she gets here at the crack of dawn and hangs around by the front door until the custodian comes and lets her in."

"I'll have to admit that it's a good idea," said Melanie. "But why does *my* mother have to be the one to do it? I mean, how will it look having our beautiful new van pull up to school with a sign on the side saying EDWARDS'S TEEN TAXI? And kids *paying* her for a ride home? I'll get laughed right out of school."

"Maybe not," said Christie, but Melanie could tell by the tone of her voice that she wasn't convinced.

"I can hear the jokes now," Melanie went on. "I mean, why couldn't she just get a regular job? And it isn't as if she has nothing to do at home, either. Jeffy only goes half-days to kindergarten. And then there's Rainbow and the puppies. They need to be let in and out during the day."

"I think you've just answered your own question," said Jana. "She can't get a regular job because she's needed at home."

Melanie squirmed, knowing Jana was right, and glanced off toward the school building, hoping she would see something interesting to take her mind off her new problem. Naturally the first place she looked was in the direction of a group of boys near the gum tree. They were eighth-graders, and her heart leapt when she saw Garrett Boldt's head above the others. Garrett was one of the tallest boys in school, as well as one of the cutest, and Melanie had been trying for a long time to figure out how to get a date with him. While she was watching, he nodded and said something to the others and then walked off alone, concentrating on juggling his books, his camera, and a camera bag as he went.

Melanie waved a quick good-bye to her friends and hurried after him. "Hi, Garrett," she called. "It looks as if you could use some help."

"Hi," he said with a big grin. "You're right. I always manage to have about three times more stuff than I can handle. On top of that, the strap on my backpack is broken so I have to carry all these things separately. Would you hold this a minute while I get organized?"

Garrett handed her the camera bag, and Melanie giggled as her knees buckled under the surprising weight. "What do you have in here?" she teased. "A bowling ball?"

"Naw. Just lenses and stuff. If you think that's bad, you should be with me when I'm shooting pictures for *The Wigwam*. Sometimes I have my tripod, or if it's an indoor shot, I might even have some portable lights. What I could really use is an assistant to help me carry all that junk."

"An assistant?" Melanie tried to control the excitement in her voice, and she could feel her pulse revving up to racing speed. "Gosh, that sounds like fun. I've always been interested in photography."

"Really?" There was an approving tone in Garrett's voice as he gave her a sideways glance. "Do you know anything about 35-millimeter cameras?"

"Not much yet," Melanie lied. Actually she knew absolutely nothing, but this was too great an opportunity to let slip by. "But I'll bet if I watched you, I could learn a lot."

"Hey, maybe you *could* be my assistant," said Garrett, nodding as if he thought the idea were perfect. "I know Mr. Neal wouldn't mind. Of course you'd have to join the yearbook staff, but that would be easy." Then his face clouded. "I don't know though. I mean, it might look awfully macho, me jumping around taking pictures and you loaded down with all my gear. You'd have to follow me around and set up my equipment and stuff like that. It would blow your friend Katie Shannon's mind."

Melanie gulped hard. "Don't worry about Katie," she insisted. "After all, you'd be teaching me all about photography, wouldn't you? There's nothing macho about being a teacher."

Garrett thought a moment. Then he nodded, as if the more he considered the idea of being her teacher, the more he liked it. "Yeah, I guess you're right. Why don't you tell Mr. Neal that you want to be on the staff and assist me with pictures, and I'll let you know the next time I have something to shoot."

"Great! I'll talk to Mr. Neal today." Melanie knew she was letting too much excitement creep into her voice, but she couldn't help it. This could be her big opportunity to make an impression on Garrett and maybe even get a date with him.

"Okay. It's a deal, assistant," he said, giving her a snappy salute.

Melanie giggled as she returned his salute and handed back his camera bag. Just then the first bell rang and they said good-bye and hurried in separate directions toward their lockers.

Assistant. She loved the way the word sounded when Garrett said it. She could hardly wait until she got the chance to start her new duties as the assistant photographer for *The Wigwam.* So what if she had to carry a ton of stuff, or gear, as Garrett called it? It would be worth it.

Melanie hung up her jacket, grabbed her books out of her locker, and headed down the hall toward her first class of the day. She had spent so much time talking to Garrett that she had missed seeing any of the other members of The Fabulous Five at their lockers and she was thinking about how she would break the news about her new job to them as she walked along.

Katie was the feminist of the group. She would

probably go into her usual routine about how Melanie was boy crazy, Melanie thought, but that was okay. As long as she didn't make a big deal about equal rights for women and how Garrett should carry his own gear. Katie was an absolute broken record about things like that.

Christie might think she was overdoing it in the boyfriend department, too, since she had decided months ago that she wasn't ready to do much dating. Christie was awfully serious about her grades.

Beth, on the other hand, was always thinking about acting and publicity. She loved having her picture taken so she would probably be thrilled to have a best friend who was the assistant photographer for the yearbook.

Jana would be happy, too. She was seventh-grade coeditor of *The Wigwam* along with Funny Hawthorne, and she was always talking about how much fun it was to work on the yearbook.

Melanie was deep in thought when she turned the corner by the principal's office and almost slammed into *her mother*!

"Mom!" she shouted, screeching to a halt less than a foot from her equally surprised mother. "What are you doing here?"

"Melanie, honey." Her mother gasped. "Hi. I didn't expect to run into you." Then she smiled and added, "No pun intended."

"Right," said Melanie. "But what are you doing here?"

Mrs. Edwards brightened. "I'm going to see Mr. Bell to talk to him about my new taxi service. I hope he'll help me get the word out to families who need the service so that I can get this new business going right away."

Melanie felt herself caving inward like a balloon with a slow leak. Not the taxi service again! she thought. Why couldn't her mother just forget it? And going to Mr. Bell, of all people. If any students overheard them talking, it would be all over Wacko by lunch period.

CHAPTER

3

*M*elanie was wrong. The first person stopped her in the hall between first and second periods.

"Is it true that your mother is starting a taxi service, of all things?" asked Laura McCall, raising her eyebrows as if she were shocked. Behind her, Tammy Lucero and Melissa McConnell giggled and exchanged knowing glances.

"She's thinking about it," scoffed Melanie. It burned her up that the others were laughing. But then, they were members of The Fantastic Foursome, arch-rivals of The Fabulous Five, and they never missed an opportunity to make life miserable for Melanie and her friends. "So what?" she challenged.

16

"It's just weird, that's all," said Laura, and behind her, the others nodded. "I mean, whoever heard of someone's mother driving a taxi to school?"

Melanie spun around and stomped off down the hall. "That's all you know!" she shouted back over her shoulder. She knew it sounded dumb, but it was all she could think to say. She had never heard of a mother taxiing kids to and from school before either, but she certainly couldn't admit that to Laura.

A couple of other kids stopped her in the cafeteria at noon, but at least they asked more politely. Jana and Christie both told her that they had had inquiries, too.

For the rest of the day Melanie waited for someone else to come up to her and make the dreaded announcement that they had heard about her mother's teen taxi. She cringed each time anyone stopped to speak to her or ask her a question, and she froze every time she heard anyone laughing behind her, afraid to turn around and find that they were laughing at her instead. And what about the teachers? What did they think? The question was on her mind when she stopped in Mr. Neal's room after lunch to talk to him about joining the yearbook staff, but if he had an opinion, he kept it to himself.

Still, what good did it really do to postpone her total embarrassment one more day? she wondered. Everyone would have to find out about it sooner or later. Unless . . . Maybe there was still time, she thought. If she could only think of a way to talk her mother out of the whole thing.

"Mom?" she called out as sweetly as she could when she got home from school in the afternoon. "Mom? Where are you? I need to talk to you."

"Up here, dear," her mother called back from upstairs. "I'm in the bedroom."

Melanie grabbed an apple from the bowl in the middle of the kitchen table and took the stairs two at a time, finding her mother sitting at her desk in the corner of the master bedroom. Papers were spread across the desk, and Mrs. Edwards was poking away at a small calculator with the eraser end of a pencil and humming under her breath. She looked up when Melanie entered the room and smiled broadly.

"More good news," she said brightly before Melanie could swallow her bite of apple and say hello. "I've been doing some figuring, and it looks as if my new business is going to be even more profitable than I had expected."

"Really?" mumbled Melanie. This certainly wasn't the way she had wanted the conversation to start.

Her mother nodded. "That's right. Mr. Bell said that in Wakeman there are approximately seventy-seven latchkey kids—you know, kids whose parents work so there's no one home to drive them—who are not eligible for bus service." She pushed her glasses up and squinted at her figures. "Now," she went on, "if I can just get five passengers at twenty-five dollars round-trip per week, that's one hundred twenty-five dollars per week altogether, less car expenses. I also might be able to take another load of five students home every day when the after-school activities let out if their parents could drop them off in the morning. If I charge them fifteen dollars a week one way, that would be another seventy-five dollars." She rose to her feet with an air of triumph and waved a finger into the air. "*Or* a cool two hundred dollars a week. Isn't that *spectacular?*"

Melanie let out her breath in one huge burst of air. It was spectacular, all right. But not at all the way her mother meant it. What was spectacular was that she was about to become the laughingstock of Wakeman Junior High so that her mother could earn a measly two hundred dollars a week.

"Now, of course it's going to take some sacrificing on everyone's part," her mother went on. "I'll have to keep my attention strictly on my driving, so I'm going to have to ask you to ride along both in the morning and after school to supervise Jeffy."

"What!" shrieked Melanie. "Ride along? After *school?* But Mom! I can't do that. I'm . . . I'm . . . I'm *busy.*"

Her mother nodded patiently. "As I said, it's

going to take some sacrificing by everyone, but in return we get a beautiful new van, and I finally get a small career. A business of my own that will let me get out of the house some of the time and still be here when I'm needed. Of course, dinner will be later in the evening. And you're going to have to miss one or two things after school. . . ."

"One or two things?" Melanie asked incredulously. "But Mom. What about cheerleading? You know we practice after school, and I just told Garrett Boldt that I'd be his photography assistant for the yearbook. Sometimes he has to shoot things after school."

"But we're between sport seasons right now, dear, and there aren't any games, so you aren't practicing as much. In fact, I've already spoken to Miss Wolfe about it. By the time your practices pick up again, we'll have something else arranged."

"Like what?" challenged Melanie. "And what about times when I have to help Garrett with a photography assignment?"

"I'm not sure yet, dear," her mother said soothingly. "But we'll work out something."

"And what about going to Bumpers after school with everyone? I'll never see my friends except in class. You'll ruin my social life!"

Mrs. Edwards stepped forward, encircling Melanie's shoulders with an arm and looking at her sympathetically. "I know it seems that way right now, sweetheart," she said softly. "But it won't be that bad. You'll see. As I said before, we'll work things out."

Not that bad? Melanie thought. How could her mother say such a thing? Here she had come home, hoping to talk her mother out of the entire business of running a teen taxi, and instead, she was losing her total social life. How would she face kids at school? And what would she tell Garrett? She'd die if he needed her after school and she couldn't be his assistant. Was her mother going to wreck that, too?

Melanie blinked and looked back at her mother, who was pacing back and forth across the bedroom, still talking up a storm. ". . . and I've even thought of adding a kindergarten run," she was saying, "except you wouldn't be available to help supervise the children, and they'd be just about as easy to control from the driver's seat as Rainbow's puppies."

Melanie's pulse quickened at the mention of the eight little dogs. They were probably snuggled up in a heap, sound asleep in their box in the basement at this very moment. She could see them now. Beth and Katie and Christie and Jana. Scott and Shane and Garrett and Jason. A pile of fat little tummies, long, floppy ears, and soft baby snores.

"What *about* Rainbow's puppies?" Melanie insisted, feeling tears spurt into her eyes. "You can't just go off and leave them alone all the time. They need to go outside sometimes and things like that." She looked at her mother pleadingly. If anything could get to her, surely this would be it.

"Why, Melanie, you know we've been planning all along to give them away. In fact, I called the newspaper this morning to put an ad in the classified section."

Her mother's words stabbed at Melanie's heart, and she sucked in her breath and ran out of the room. She flew down the stairs to the first floor, ignored Jeffy, who called out to her from the kitchen table where he was coloring, and plunged into the basement. In the dim light of the overhead bulb she could see the eight tiny puppies, heaped together and sound asleep, just as she had known they would be. They were beautiful, and she loved them so much that she thought her heart would burst.

"Oh, Rainbow," she whispered, cupping the mother dog's face in her hands and looking into her gentle, trusting eyes. "What are we going to do?"

CHAPTER

4

$\mathcal{B}$y the next morning Melanie had a plan. Sabotage. Plain and simple. She would talk to kids who were potential customers and convince them not to sign up. The night before she had overheard her mother talking on the phone to the parents of three Wacko students, Shawnie Pendergast, Kevin Walker-Noles, and Michelle Troyer. Melanie knew that there had to be more families her mother was planning to contact, but at least she had somewhere to start. She would try to catch each of them alone, since she dreaded bringing up the subject of the taxi in public. She wished she didn't have to talk about the taxi at all, but she didn't see that she had much choice.

"Hi, Shawnie," she called as she sauntered onto the school ground and saw Shawnie Pendergast lingering by a tree. "Has my mother called your parents about her new taxi service?"

"She sure has," said Shawnie, bursting into a grin. "My mom's pretty excited about it. And so am I. It means I get to sleep another half-hour every morning."

Melanie took a deep breath and crossed her fingers behind her back. Shawnie was playing right into her hands. "Well, with my mom driving, you'll certainly be awake by the time you get to school."

Shawnie cocked an eyebrow and looked at Melanie. "What do you mean?" she asked slowly.

"Oh, nothing," said Melanie with a shrug. "It's just that it's a real adventure riding with my mom. Don't tell *your* mom, though. Okay? She probably wouldn't let you ride if she knew what kind of driver my mom is."

She left Shawnie standing in the middle of the school ground with a strange look on her face. This is working, she thought gleefully. The next person she looked for was Kevin Walker-Noles. He was definitely a candidate for the taxi service. He had hated being a latchkey kid so much that he had harassed Christie on the homework hot line just to get attention. She knew he rode his bike to school, but his parents were doing everything they could for him now that they understood his problem.

She found Kevin locking his bike into the rack by the side of the building. "Hi, Kev," she said, trying to sound casual.

"Oh, hi, Melanie," he said, snapping the lock in place and walking toward her. "Guess I won't be doing this much longer," he added, nodding toward his bike. "I'll probably start riding with your mom."

"Really?" Melanie concentrated on putting a worried expression on her face. "What's your first class in the morning?"

"Biology. Why?"

Melanie shook her head. "Wow. That's too bad. You'd better explain to Mr. Dracovitch that you'll probably be late most mornings. My mom's never been on time a day in her life."

"Late?" Kevin burst out. "I can't be late to biology. Besides, homeroom comes before first period. There's no way your mom would be that late."

"You don't know my mom," said Melanie.

She spotted Michelle Troyer sitting alone on the steps a few minutes later. Michelle was terribly shy and never spoke up in class and never *never* talked to boys. Taking a deep breath, Melanie approached her.

"Hi, Michelle," she called out. "I heard my mom

talking to your mom last night. Are you going to ride in the teen taxi?"

Michelle nodded, but she didn't say anything.

"Great," said Melanie, plastering a big grin on her face. "It's going to be a blast. The way Mom's signing up riders, we'll be packed in like sardines. I wouldn't be surprised if we end up sitting on each other's lap, but that's okay. She's signed up mostly boys."

Melanie felt a twinge of guilt as the color drained out of Michelle's face. "Boys?" Michelle whispered.

"Right," said Melanie. "Hunks from the football team and a bunch of other cute guys. I can't wait, can you?"

"Um . . . I'll see you later," Michelle stammered as she got to her feet and gathered her books in her arms. "I have to go to my locker."

Melanie's friends were already at their usual meeting spot by the fence, so after she left Michelle she hurried to them, telling herself that even though the things she had told Shawnie, Kevin, and Michelle were big fat lies, she had had to do it.

"How's baby Jana and the rest of the puppies?" Jana asked the minute she walked up.

"Okay, but Mom said the ad to give them away will be in the paper tonight." Melanie moaned. "I just can't *stand* the idea. Poor little Christie and Beth and Jana and Katie and Scott and Shane and Garrett and Jason!" she said, all in one breath. Gulping in more air, she went on, "How will we know if the people who take them will be good to them? I've read awful stories about people getting pets and then mistreating them."

"Maybe you won't be able to give them away," offered Beth. "Remember how much trouble we had finding homes for the dogs and cats from the animal shelter?"

"And all of those animals were paper trained and had their shots," added Jana.

"Maybe you're right," Melanie mumbled. "But Mom's going ahead full steam with her taxi business just as if she already had homes for the puppies. She got the sign put on both sides of the van yesterday and spent all evening making calls to parents who might want to use her service."

"How many riders did she get?" asked Katie.

Melanie shrugged. "I didn't ask. Believe me, it's the last thing in the world I want to talk about. But I did overhear her telling Dad that she wants to start up her taxi service next Monday morning."

"Wow," said Christie. "This is Thursday. That doesn't give you much time. Does it?"

Melanie smiled slyly. "Maybe, and maybe not. I've been doing some work on my own."

Her friends looked at her quizzically.

"You know how my mom drives," she said.

"Yeah," said Beth, nodding her head and laughing. "She certainly doesn't poke around."

"Exactly," said Melanie. "She's always above the speed limit. And you also know how often she's running late. Well," she said slowly, ". . . I've just been spreading the word to kids who might sign up for the taxi service, among other things."

"Melanie! You haven't," shrieked Katie.

Melanie nodded and grinned at her friend. "What's wrong with that? I didn't lie. At least, not very much. And besides, they ought to know what they're getting into."

"I don't know," said Christie. "I'm not sure you should have done that."

"Me, either," said Jana. "You know your mother takes her responsibility seriously. She's never driven dangerously. I'm sure she'll stay under the speed limit and always be on time with her new taxi service."

Melanie sighed and shook her head woefully. "But I already told you about having to ride along after school," she wailed. "I can just see all of you going to Bumpers every day without me. I keep seeing pictures in my mind of other girls flirting with Scott, Shane, and Garrett." Her eyes narrowed in anger. "I've got to do something."

"We'll call you every night and tell you what hap-

pened at Bumpers," Christie offered sympathetically.

"And if we see anybody flirting with those guys,
we'll do our best to break it up," promised Beth.

Melanie was glad when the bell rang. She didn't
want to talk to her friends anymore about her
predicament. They didn't understand how it felt.
Their mothers weren't wrecking everything by embarrassing them at school, messing up their social
lives, and giving away eight of the sweetest puppies
ever born. She would just have to handle the problem on her own.

CHAPTER

5

*O*n Sunday night Melanie tossed and turned in bed, imagining what it would be like to arrive at school the next morning. Would kids laugh when the van saying EDWARDS'S TEEN TAXI pulled up to the curb and other kids got out? Would they snicker behind her back when she walked through the halls and make jokes about her mother's being a taxi driver?

When she came down to breakfast the next morning Mrs. Edwards was sitting by the phone, frowning and tapping her fingers on the kitchen counter.

"I've just had another cancellation," she said in an agitated voice. "I don't understand it. I had four students lined up to ride today, and three of their parents have called and canceled. And when I asked them why, they hemmed and hawed and wouldn't really give me a reason."

Melanie's eyes widened. "Really?" she asked, faking concern. Little tingles raced up her spine. Her campaign to sabotage the taxi service had worked. Now surely her mother would give up if no one wanted their children to ride.

"At least we still have one customer," said Mrs. Edwards with a sigh. "But I'll need to find more if this taxi business is going to succeed. We'll never be able to make the van payments with only one rider."

Melanie knew she shouldn't feel so jubilant. Her mother really wanted to make her new business work, not just for herself, but for the whole family's benefit as well. But why couldn't she start a business selling her fabulous homemade brownies instead? she wondered. She might get rich. Look what had happened with Famous Amos's cookies, or Ben and Jerry's ice cream.

"Hurry with your breakfast, dear," her mother called, interrupting her thoughts. "We'll need to leave in ten minutes."

Melanie's optimistic mood vanished, and she scowled after her mother, who hurried off to get Jeffy ready for the trip. Melanie couldn't even make something as easy as toast and get it eaten in ten minutes. It was just one more example of what was wrong with running a taxi service. Her mother was more interested in her career than in her daughter's nutrition!

She downed a fast glass of milk and stuffed the last bite of a banana into her mouth as she climbed into the van ten minutes later.

Her mother looked up from buckling Jeffy into the front passenger seat and said, "Now, honey, don't forget that you are in charge of your little brother beginning the instant the young man steps into our van."

"Young man?" Melanie echoed, sliding into the seat directly behind her mother, her interest suddenly piqued. Perhaps she should have asked more about her mother's riders after all.

"Yes," said her mother as she started up the engine, backed out of the driveway, and headed down the street. "I'll need your help watching for his street, too. It's Pebblestone Road. His mother said it is four blocks south of here and six blocks west. Then it's the fifth house on the left . . . JEFFY!"

Melanie gasped as her little brother popped the buckle on his seat belt and rolled out of his seat, heading for the back of the moving van as fast as he could scramble. Just as Melanie leaned forward to grab him, her mother pulled to the curb and hit the brakes, sending her lurching onto the carpeted floor beside Jeffy.

"Jeffy! You get back in your seat!" shouted Mrs. Edwards. Then she turned her glare on Melanie. "You were supposed to be helping me. Now we can't have things like this happening while we have passengers in the van. Get into the front seat, please, and hold Jeffy on your lap."

"Mu-*THUR*!" cried Melanie as she scrambled around on her hands and knees gathering books and papers that had tumbled onto the floor. "You said I was supposed to start watching him as soon as the passenger got in. Besides, I can't ride up to the school in front of everybody with Jeffy on my lap. Come on, Mom! I'll watch him. I promise!"

Her mother shook her head firmly. "I can't take any chances. This taxi service is a big responsibility, and Jeffy could cause an accident. You simply have to hold him in your lap at all times."

"Oooooh," Melanie groaned as she sat down hard in the tall, chairlike seat next to her mother and jerked Jeffy onto her lap. "You sit still or I'll kill you," she mumbled into his ear. Then she snapped the seat belt across both of them and took a deep breath to calm herself.

"There it is. Pebblestone Road," her mother chirped a moment later.

Melanie barely glanced up as the big van swung left onto the street because Jeffy was kicking her shins and trying to wriggle out of her lap.

"Jeffy. I said to sit still," she said through clenched teeth.

"I want *down*," he insisted, planting an elbow firmly in her stomach.

"You know what you're going to get?" she challenged. "You're going to get me sitting on *your* lap, if you're not careful," she warned. "Then let's see you move even so much as an inch."

She shot an angry look at her mother, who was totally absorbed in reading house numbers and oblivious to what was going on between Melanie and Jeffy. Why didn't *she* take care of Jeffy? Melanie wondered. Wasn't that what mothers were supposed to do? She opened her mouth to say so when Mrs. Edwards abruptly sat up straight behind the wheel and called out triumphantly, "There it is. Fourteen-oh-seven Pebblestone Road." Then she swung the van into the driveway and beamed at Melanie. "And here comes our first rider."

Melanie heard the van door slide open on its tracks, and she started to turn around to see who was getting in, but Jeffy picked that moment to try to squeeze himself upward and out of her grip. She tightened her arms around him and pulled him back into her lap, growling, "Don't you dare!" in as mean a voice as she could muster.

Just then the door slammed shut again and Melanie half-turned to see a hulking form sink into the seat directly behind her. Then a huge face loomed toward her that was wearing an idiotic grin.

"Hi, Melanie! Hey, this is great! You and me! Riding to school together!"

Her heart stopped. The rider was Brian Olsen.

CHAPTER

6

*I*f this is a nightmare, please let me wake up, Melanie pleaded silently as her mother stopped the van squarely in front of Wakeman Junior High. Over Jeffy's bobbing head she could see students standing in clusters or walking in ones and twos, all acting as if this were a perfectly normal day and that everything in the world were okay. But it wasn't, not for Melanie anyway.

What am I going to do? she thought. Over her shoulder she could see Brian Olsen getting to his feet as she unbuckled the seat belt and let Jeffy off her lap. Brian was still grinning that same idiotic grin he'd had on his face when he got into the van fifteen minutes ago, and she wouldn't have been the least bit surprised if he'd started slobbering all over her.

"Come on, Melanie. We're *here*!" he shouted as if he had just given her the greatest news on earth. "Let's get out."

Brian stretched an arm toward her, and Melanie had the split-second impression that he was going to scoop her up—the way King Kong scoops up Fay Wray in the movie—and carry her off. Maybe he'd even make his way up to the roof of the school with her in his arms and wait for airplanes to attack. But to her immense relief, he only motioned for her to follow him.

"Come on," he insisted. "What are you waiting for?"

"Umm, I have to talk to my mom for a minute," she said quickly.

Brian raked his fingers through his short blond hair as if he were thinking the idea over. Then he grinned broadly again and nodded. "Okay. See you around," he called as he lumbered out of the van.

"Not if I see you first," Melanie mumbled too softly for her mother to hear.

"What is it, honey?" her mother asked brightly. "What did you want to talk to me about?"

"Oh," said Melanie. "Well, umm, nothing really. I'd better run."

"Okay, but don't forget that I'll be here after

school to drive him home and I'll need you to help with your little brother again."

"Oh, Mom," Melanie pleaded. "Can't you let him play at a friend's house or something? Or maybe Mrs. Miller would keep him for a few minutes. I really wanted to go to Bumpers with my friends."

"I'm sorry, honey, but I really *need* you to help me. I'll be right out here when the dismissal bell rings. See you then."

Melanie barely answered. How could her mother do this to her? Sliding out of the van, she pulled the door shut and checked to see which way Brian Olsen had gone. She wouldn't go that way herself, no matter what. As she turned to find her friends, she noticed that several kids had stopped and were staring in her direction. She panicked. Were they looking at the van? Were they reading the taxi sign on the side and thinking how weird it was for a student's mother to do a thing like that? Or were they too busy noticing that the biggest moron in Wacko had just ridden to school with *her*? Whichever it was, she wanted to get out of there before the laughing started.

She was breathless when she reached her friends at the fence.

"So how did it go?" asked Jana.

"We saw Brian Olsen getting out of the van," Beth said sympathetically. "Of all the rotten luck."

"You can say that again," huffed Melanie. "Half the school must have seen him. You should have seen the stares I got. It was awful."

"Is he your mom's only rider?" asked Christie.

Melanie nodded. "I scared off all the rest of them, but I didn't know about Brian."

"Speak of the devil," said Katie, nodding in the direction of the sidewalk. "I think he's headed this way."

"Hey, Melanie," Brian called as if on cue. "Come here a minute. I want to talk to you."

Melanie felt as if her knees were going to buckle. Brian was practically shouting, and other kids were stopping to see what was going on.

"Hey, Melanie!" he shouted again before she had figured out what to do. "Hey, I want to ask you something."

Brian was moving closer to The Fabulous Five, and more kids were stopping to stare. Melanie felt the hair rising on the back of her neck. There was nothing to do but talk to him, and she would have to do it fast before the entire student body was looking at them.

"Sure, Brian. I'll be right there," she said quickly. She looked at the ground as she hurried toward him, not wanting to look anyone in the eye.

"So, what do you want?" she asked impatiently as she looked up at him. "Are you canceling out on my mom's taxi service or something?"

"Gosh, no," he said, grinning broadly. "What I wanted to ask you is if you think she'd mind if I brought a bunch of bricks along in the morning?" He squinted thoughtfully. "Maybe a dozen, fifteen bricks. Do you think she'd have any objection to carrying them in the van? I'll make sure that they aren't dirty."

Melanie stared at him openmouthed. Then she screwed up her face and asked, "*Bricks?* Why on earth would you want to bring bricks to school?"

"Actually, I may need to bring some boards, too," he said thoughtfully. "But I'll definitely need to bring bricks. They're for a karate demonstration I'm giving at the school assembly tomorrow. Did you know that I'm a brown belt and that I can smash bricks with my bare hands?"

His eyes were gleaming as he grinned at her, and she felt a queasy sensation in the pit of her stomach. "Smash bricks?" she whispered, unable to believe the words.

"You bet," said Brian proudly. "Actually, I can smash concrete blocks, but they shatter and make a bigger mess than bricks. Hey, I've got an idea. Would you like to come onstage with me and be my assistant?"

A snicker from nearby jolted Melanie, and she looked around. To her horror, a crowd was gathering and kids were listening to their conversation, and right in the center stood The Fabulous Five's arch-rivals, The Fantastic Foursome. Tammy Lucero, Melissa McConnell, and Funny Hawthorne were standing around Laura McCall, who looked as if she were having the time of her life at Melanie's expense.

"Go ahead, Mel," called out Alexis Duvall. "Maybe you can wear a cute little short skirt like they do on TV."

Some other kids burst out laughing at that, and Melanie wanted to die. She knew that Alexis was only joking, but this was no joking matter. And to say it in front of The Fantastic Foursome only made things worse.

"Thanks, Brian, but . . . but loud noises give me a headache," she offered with a shrug. It was a lame excuse, but it was the best she could do under the circumstances. He looked disappointed so she added, "You can talk to my mom about the bricks. Okay?"

When Brian had gone and most of the other kids had wandered off, leaving Melanie and her friends standing alone, she sighed deeply. "A karate demon-stration smashing bricks. Can you believe that?" she said. Then she looked pleadingly at each of her friends and added, "Somebody help me think of something to do about him. I have a terrible feeling that this is only going to get worse."

CHAPTER

7

By now everyone at school knew about the teen taxi. Kids came up to Melanie everywhere she went. But instead of asking her the question she had expected—how does it feel to have a mother who runs a taxi service to and from Wakeman Junior High?—they all wanted to know about Brian Olsen.

"How can you let a drip like that ride with you every day?" asked Mona Vaughn, stopping Melanie outside her English class. "I mean, doesn't your mother screen kids or anything?"

"No," Melanie grumbled. "She'll let anybody ride if they pay the money."

"But Brian Olsen!" protested Sara Sawyer, who

had walked up just in time to hear Mona's question. "He's such a Neanderthal."

"Tell me about it," Melanie said with a sigh.

At lunchtime it was even worse. Funny Hawthorne came sailing up to The Fabulous Five's table carrying her hot-lunch tray out in front of her. Then she bent down and whispered something to Jana, who rolled her eyes and made a face.

"What was that all about?" asked Beth.

Jana looked at Melanie as if she hated to speak, but then she said, "Funny said Joel Murphy and Clarence Marshall are giving Scott Daly a hard time about Brian's riding to school with Melanie."

"What!" shrieked Melanie, rising up off the bench and dropping her sandwich.

"Calm down," said Christie. "You know how boys are. Besides, if they see that they're getting to you, they'll tease him more than ever."

Melanie sank back to her seat, but she didn't pick up her sandwich. She couldn't eat. Not if one of the boys she liked was getting teased over Brian Olsen. Actually, she had liked Scott longer than any of the other boys she had crushes on, which made him special. She was going to have to do something about Brian and do it fast, before her entire love life went down the drain.

"Maybe your mom won't let Brian bring bricks in

the van tomorrow, and he'll have to find another ride," offered Katie.

"Fat chance," scoffed Melanie. "She's so desperate for riders that she would probably let him bring a baby elephant, if he had one."

"What about the stuff you told the other kids?" suggested Jana. "You know, about your mother's being a reckless driver and always being late?"

"No, Brian would never fall for that," said Melanie, shaking her head. "He's already ridden with Mom once. She was a model driver, and she got to his house exactly on time."

"There has to be something you can do to get rid of him," said Christie. "You're such an expert on getting boys to notice you. You've even memorized seven tips for flirting. Don't you know anything about reversing the whole thing?"

"Yeah," said Jana. "How do you turn guys *off*?"

Melanie bit her lower lip and thought over Jana's question. It was true, she had made it practically a lifetime project to learn how to attract boys. And Christie was right about the seven tips for flirting, too. She had not only memorized them, she could even say them backward. But never once in her whole life had it ever occurred to her to get a boy to *stop* liking her. She hadn't considered the possibility that she would ever want to do a thing like that.

"Wow," she said just above a whisper. "I don't

have the faintest idea, but if there are ways to get guys, surely there are ways to get rid of them, too."

"Let's think about this. Maybe we could help," said Katie. "After all, The Fabulous Five sticks together. We could ask some boys what girls do that bug them the most, especially things that would make them stop having a crush on someone. I'll ask Tony, if you want me to."

"Great idea," chimed in Jana. "I'll ask Randy."

Melanie's eyes got wide with excitement. "I could even ask some guys myself," she said. "In fact," she added with a twinkle, "it's the kind of information that we ought to have anyway. Who knows when somebody else might need it?"

The girls finished their lunches talking about how they would approach all the boys they knew really well and ask them to name their biggest complaints against girls.

"Not just silly stuff, but stuff that keeps them from asking girls out," Katie reminded them.

"As soon as we get a list made, I'll try every single one of them on Brian Olsen!" Melanie vowed. "If that doesn't get rid of him, nothing will."

The first boy Melanie talked to was Shane Arrington. He was in her biology class right after lunch, and they walked into the room at the same time.

"Shane, what do girls do sometimes that bugs you the most?" she asked.

Shane looked thoughtful for a moment and then said, "What really bugs me is when girls gossip. I really hate to hear them saying nasty things about other girls."

"Oh, yeah?" she said casually, making a mental note to write his reply in her notebook. That was actually a useful thing to know about Shane, even if she didn't have a problem with Brian Olsen. She would be extra careful not to say anything bad about *anybody* when she was around Shane from now on.

Next she stopped at the drinking fountain between classes and talked to Curtis Trowbridge. "Say, Curtis, what do girls do sometimes that really makes you mad enough not to like them anymore?"

"Who, me?" said Curtis, as if he couldn't imagine anyone's asking him a question like that. "Well, probably what I hate most is when they talk about other guys. You know, how handsome they are, what jocks they are, things like that," he answered with an embarrassed smile.

Melanie couldn't help feeling a little embarrassed, too. Curtis certainly wasn't handsome. And he wasn't a jock. What he was, was a genius, and fellow-genius Whitney Larkin was the only girl Melanie knew of who had ever liked him for a boyfriend. But still, she couldn't imagine anyone being mean enough to talk about how much of a hunk someone else was in front of Curtis.

Between her next two classes, Melanie spotted Garrett Boldt in the hallway. She couldn't believe her good luck. In fact, it was perfect. It would give her a chance to start up a conversation with him, which she had been dying to do ever since he had agreed for her to be his assistant. She could also get some information she could use to get rid of Brian.

She looked around nervously. Garrett was an eighth-grader and a lot more sophisticated than the other boys she had talked to. What could she say? *Hi, Garrett. What bugs you most about girls?* Eeek! she thought. He'll think I've lost my mind. *Hi, Garrett. If you liked a girl a lot, what would she have to do for you to change your mind?* No, that wouldn't do either.

I'll just have to wing it, she thought desperately as she raced down the hall after him.

"Hi, Garrett," she called. "Wait up."

"Oh, hi, Mel," he said, giving her a friendly smile and slowing down until she caught up. "How's it going?"

"Great," she said. "By the way, I'm doing a project for social studies," she lied, hoping her face wasn't as red as it felt. She could never tell a lie without blushing. Not even a teensy white lie. "I was wondering if you'd answer a question for me."

"Sure," said Garrett.

Melanie nibbled on her lower lip and then plunged on. "If you could name the one thing that would make you stop liking a girl, what would it be?"

Garrett looked at her quizzically for a moment. "Must be a new project this year," he said. "I don't remember anything like that last year."

"Oh, it's new all right," she assured him. "And really interesting. I'll tell you more about it later."

"Okay," he said, nodding. "Now back to the question. I guess the one thing that bothers me most is when a girl reneges on a promise. I really hate it when she says she'll do something and then she doesn't do it. I don't know why some girls are like that. Do you?"

"Gosh, no," said Melanie. "That's awful. I mean, when you make a promise, you should keep it. I can see why that would bother you."

Garrett nodded and then glanced around at the dwindling crowd in the hall. "Gotta go," he said, taking off at a run. "The bell's going to ring any second. Hey, but Mel," he called back over his shoulder. "I just remembered. I'm supposed to shoot some pictures of the drama club's rehearsal tomorrow after school. Meet me in the yearbook room right after the bell. Okay, assistant?"

"Sure," she called after him, almost choking on the word. Tomorrow after school? She watched him disappear into a classroom, wishing she could crawl into a hole in the wall and hide. She had really blown it now. What was she going to do? How could she tell him that she had to ride in her mother's teen taxi every day after school? After what he had just said to her, how could she possibly explain that she was going to renege on her promise?

CHAPTER

8

"We'll walk you out to the taxi," offered Christie. She and the rest of The Fabulous Five had gathered at Melanie's locker after school and were giving her sympathetic looks.

"Thanks, guys," Melanie said. "You're really good friends."

Katie chuckled and linked an arm through Melanie's. "Hey, we're The Fabulous Five," she said. "And we promise to talk to the guys at Bumpers and let you know what they say about turnoffs."

Melanie nodded gratefully. "Let's not hurry to the van," she said, ambling slowly down the hall toward the door. "I know my mom is probably already parked out front in the bus zone, but if I stall awhile, maybe most kids will already be gone when we get out there. The fewer people who see me get into the taxi with Brian Olsen, the better."

"Sara Sawyer told me he was bragging in social studies class about how great it was to have his own private taxi," said Beth.

Melanie sighed. "That's just part of it," she said. "I saw him twice between classes today, and once he yelled, 'Hey, Mel. See you at the taxi stand!' Isn't that gross? I wanted to die."

When they got outside, Melanie saw that she had not stalled long enough. Tons of kids were still lingering on the front lawn. A few of the buses were gone, but several were still loading. And there, in the midst of them all, was her mother's big blue van with EDWARDS'S TEEN TAXI on the side.

"We'll call you and tell you if anything exciting happens at Bumpers," Jana promised, and the others nodded.

"Thanks. I'll see you guys later," Melanie said, and headed toward the van. At least she didn't see Brian anywhere. Maybe his locker door was stuck, she thought hopefully. No. If that happened, he would just tear it off its hinges. Maybe he had to stay late to talk to a teacher. Or maybe he even went out the wrong door and was wandering around behind the school looking for the van. The last idea made her laugh. Who cares? she thought. Anything to keep him from showing up with lots of kids around and doing something dumb.

She was almost to the van when a movement above her head caught her attention. Flinching, she looked up in time to see Brian Olsen dropping out of a nearby tree. Except he didn't drop all the way to the ground. He grabbed hold of a high branch with both hands and grinned at her.

"Hey, Mel. Want to see me chin myself one hundred times?" he shouted. Without waiting for her to answer, he began pulling himself up and down, up and down, while she stood there with her mouth open.

She couldn't believe it. His face was practically a blur, but there he went, up and down, up and down, looking straight at her with an idiotic grin on his face.

"What's that maniac doing?" she heard someone ask behind her.

Melanie didn't wait to hear an answer. Her face was already flaming with humiliation. Sliding the van door open, she ducked inside and sank into the nearest seat. Her mother was digging in her purse and apparently didn't even notice what was going on. Melanie sighed. She couldn't stand to think how many kids were watching Brian behaving like a chimpanzee. How would she ever face anyone again?

At that same instant her little brother went streaking past her. He bounded out of the van and started bouncing up and down on the sidewalk and pointing at Brian. "Look, Mom! Look, Melanie! Look at big Brian!"

First Melanie wanted to cry. Then she wanted to shout at Jeffy to shut up, but it was too late. His shrill little voice could probably be heard for a block in any direction, and anyone who might otherwise have missed Brian Olsen's chinning demonstration would know about it now.

"Wow! You're really strong," Jeffy called out as he followed Brian into the van a moment later.

Brian dropped onto the bench seat at the back of the van and pulled Jeffy up beside him. "You really think so?" he asked, winking at Melanie.

Jeffy was nodding his head vigorously and gazing up at Brian Olsen in openmouthed admiration. "Wow!" he kept saying. "Wow, boy. Wow." Then an idea brightened his face and he shouted, "I'm going to sit with big Brian instead of Melanie. Okay, Mom?"

"That was very impressive, Brian," called Mrs. Edwards from the driver's seat, and Melanie guessed that she had looked up in time to see part of Brian's chinning demonstration. "And yes, Jeffy, you may sit with Brian as long as you fasten your seat belt."

Melanie didn't realize that she was still staring at Brian until he looked at her and asked, "And what did you think, Melanie? I chinned myself one hundred and five times instead of just one hundred."

Fortunately for Melanie, her mother chose that instant to start the van's engine so that he wouldn't have heard her answer even if she'd managed to give him one. Instead, she shot him a weak smile and swiveled her chair around to face the front of the van, busying herself with her own seat belt.

The ride to Brian's house was uneventful, and when the van pulled up to a stop in his driveway, he hurried past her and began talking to her mother.

"Mrs. Edwards," he began, "I was wondering if it would be all right if I brought ten or fifteen bricks along in the van in the morning. I promise that they won't mess up the van. You see, I need them because I'm giving a karate demonstration at an all-school assembly tomorrow."

Melanie groaned inwardly. She had forgotten all about the bricks. But her mother was looking at him with almost as much admiration on her face as Jeffy had.

"Why, of course," she insisted. "That would be just fine. I wish I could come to the assembly and see your demonstration."

Brian thanked her, and Melanie breathed a sigh of relief when he jumped out and slid the door shut behind himself with no more than a good-bye wave to her.

"I *like* big Brian," Jeffy cried, diving headlong into the front passenger seat.

"I like him, too," said Mrs. Edwards. "He's an extremely nice young man and *so strong!*"

Melanie helped Jeffy get his seat belt fastened, thinking that she didn't dare open her mouth, because if she did, she might not be able to keep from saying how *she* felt about Brian Olsen. Besides that, things were going from bad to worse. Not only had Brian completely won over her mother, but he was embarrassing the living daylights out of her in front of the kids at school. And then there was Garrett. Because of Brian, she was going to have to tell him that she couldn't be his assistant tomorrow after school, knowing that he didn't like girls who reneged on promises. She sighed and leaned back against the seat, closing her eyes. Maybe once she talked to her friends on the phone she would start to feel better again.

Then her mother reminded Melanie of the other terrible problem she still had to face. "I'm anxious to get home and see if anyone calls about the puppies," Mrs. Edwards said in a cheery voice. "The ad to give them away is supposed to start running in today's paper."

CHAPTER

9

*T*he phone was ringing when Melanie entered the house. She glanced over her shoulder and back out into the garage where her mother had parked the van and was busy helping Jeffy out of his seat belt.

I'm the only one who heard it, she thought, racing to grab it before it rang again. What if it's someone about the puppies? What will I say?

Her heart was pounding as she put the receiver to her ear. "Hello," she said softly.

"Hi, Melanie. It's Brian. Is your mother there? I forgot to ask her if I could bring some boards in the morning, too."

Melanie rolled her eyes toward the ceiling. Bricks.

56

Boards. We have a van, not a pickup truck! she wanted to shout.

Just then her mother came into the kitchen. "Oh, is it about the puppies?" she asked.

"No, it's Brian Olsen," answered Melanie. "He wants to ask you something."

Mrs. Edwards took the phone and began talking to Brian in a sugary voice that made Melanie want to throw up. What is it about parents? she wondered as she stomped off to her room. They are always crazy about boys that no girl in her right mind can stand. Brian Olsen is the biggest imbecile in the world, and my mother thinks he's wonderful.

She dropped her books on her bed and then hurried down to the basement, grabbing an armload of puppies for their afternoon outing. Being with them would make her feel better, even if nothing else would.

"Hi, Katie and Scott and Jason," she said, giving each of them a kiss on the head as she scampered up the stairs. The puppies all responded by wriggling in her arms and trying to lick her chin. She hurried back down for another load and brought up Jana and Christie and Garrett this time. Carrying Beth and Shane on her final trip out of the basement, she heard the phone ring again, and she pulled her arms tighter around the little dogs and hurried out into the yard.

Kneeling in the grass, she looked first at little Katie, whose red coat gave her a strong resemblance to an Irish setter. Katie was prancing around in the tummy-high grass with a twig in her mouth. Suddenly solid-white Jason lunged at her from the side and tried to grab the twig. Melanie giggled as they engaged in a game of tug-of-war, pulling on the twig and growling tiny little growls at each other. Plop! Katie sat down hard, opening her mouth and losing the twig to Jason, who dropped it also when he realized the game was over.

"Oh, Katie, what am I going to do if someone wants you?" Melanie said softly. She picked up the pup and cradled it against her neck. "I just love you so much. You and all your brothers and sisters."

She felt a tug on her foot and burst out laughing when she saw Jana pulling on her shoelace.

"Melanie," her mother called from the back door. "You have a phone call."

"Coming, Mom," she yelled back.

When she got to the kitchen, her mother gave her a stern look. "Don't tie up the line for too long, sweetheart. You know we're expecting calls on the ad for the puppies."

Melanie nodded, but secretly she hoped that her call would last for hours and hours so that anyone wanting to phone about the puppies would have to give up.

"Hi, Mel." It was Jana. "Somebody at Bumpers said that Brian Olsen was doing chin-ups on a tree branch by the van. Is it *true*?"

Melanie sighed. "It's true," she admitted. "I was hoping it wouldn't get back to everybody in Bumpers."

"Well, it did. And of course Tammy Lucero and Laura McCall were the ones spreading it."

"Those two!" Melanie said between gritted teeth. "Leave it to them." Then she went on to describe for Jana how Brian had swung down from the tree and had done one hundred five chin-ups in front of everyone.

"Who does he think he is, Tarzan?" Jana muttered.

Melanie laughed in spite of herself. "I can see it now," she said. "Brian, barefoot and dressed in a loincloth, giving a Tarzan yell and swinging across the cafeteria on a vine."

"Melanie," came a voice from behind her. "Remember what I said about keeping your conversation short."

"Okay, Mom," Melanie called back. "I'll be off in a minute." Then she whispered into the receiver, "Talk as long as you want to. Talk *forever*. Mom put the ad in the paper today to give away the puppies and she's waiting for calls."

"Well, I do have something else to tell you," said Jana. "Randy said he doesn't like girls who are insincere. But that doesn't surprise me," she added, "since he's the kindest and most sincere guy in the world. Oh, yeah. One more thing. Garrett came over to our table at Bumpers, and he was saying that you are supposed to help him shoot pictures for the yearbook after school tomorrow. Doesn't he know that you have to ride in the teen taxi every day after school?"

"You didn't tell him, did you?" Melanie burst out.

"Of course not, but what are you going to do?"

"I don't know yet," Melanie confessed. "And to make matters worse, I asked him what bugs him the most about girls, and he said girls who renege on promises. If I say I can't be his assistant, he'll think I'm reneging and he won't like me anymore. Then he'll *never* ask me out."

"Wow. You really do have problems, don't you?" said Jana. "The teen taxi, Brian Olsen, the puppies, and now Garrett. I wish I could be more help."

"You can," said Melanie as she was hit by a sudden burst of inspiration. "Call the rest of The Fabulous Five and ask them to start calling me. Tell them that if the line's busy, to keep on trying so that we tie it up all evening. Even if you guys can't do anything about the taxi or Brian or Garrett, at least maybe you can help me save the puppies."

"Great idea," said Jana. "I'll hang up now and call

the others. And Mel. Don't worry. The Fabulous Five can't lose."

Melanie took a deep breath as she hung up, too. Jana was right about The Fabulous Five. At least things had always worked out super in the past when they had stuck together. She would have to keep her fingers crossed that it would be the same now that she needed their help so badly.

An instant later the phone rang again. Melanie stared fearfully at it and then reached out to pick up the receiver. Oh, please, she prayed silently. Let it be one of my friends.

"Hello?" she said just above a whisper.

"Hello," came a woman's voice. "I'm calling about the ad for the puppies."

Tears shot into Melanie's eyes, and she handed the phone to her mother.

CHAPTER

10

 $\boldsymbol{\mathcal{I}}$n desperation, later that evening Melanie volunteered to tuck Jeffy into bed so that she could talk to him in private. Maybe her parents would reconsider giving away the puppies if Jeffy turned on the tears, she thought.

"But I don't want them anymore," he answered matter-of-factly.

"Why not?" asked Melanie incredulously. Jeffy loved the puppies. Surely he didn't mean that.

"Because," he said emphatically, "I was holding the brown and black one yesterday, and he peed in my hand. YUK! YUK!"

Melanie threw up her hands in frustration and

told Jeffy good-night. What else can possibly go wrong? she asked herself.

By the time Melanie went to bed, four people had called about the puppies. Two had said they weren't sure if they wanted to see the little dogs; one said he was looking for a purebred cocker spaniel; and one made an appointment to stop by the next evening.

Fortunately for Melanie, her friends had called, too.

"Just think, maybe lots more people would have been able to get through to your parents if we weren't calling," said Beth.

Melanie knew Beth was trying to cheer her up, but it wasn't working.

"By the way, do you want to know what Keith said when I asked him what he dislikes most about girls?"

"Of course," cried Melanie.

"Well, Keith says that he really hates girls who have a superior attitude. You know, girls who act as if they know everything and they think everybody else is stupid."

"Thanks," said Melanie. "That's a big help."

After she and Beth hung up, Melanie waited anxiously for Katie and Christie to call so that she could add what they had found out from boys to her list. Katie said that Tony Calcaterra couldn't stand for girls to point out his faults and bad habits. Katie had giggled when she told Melanie that, and Melanie had chuckled herself, thinking how many times Tony had appeared before Teen Court. People were constantly pointing out Tony's faults and bad habits.

Christie reported that Jon Smith didn't like girls who were always talking about their diets. He said that he thought they were really just fishing for compliments and trying to get him to tell them how cute they were.

Melanie tried to think about her list instead of the puppies as she got ready for school the next morning. She had added Keith's, Tony's, Jon's, and Randy's pet peeves to the ones she had gotten from Shane, Curtis, and Garrett. Saying nasty things about other girls, talking about other guys, reneging on promises, superior attitude, pointing out faults and bad habits, talking about diets, and being insincere. Surely one of those would discourage Brian Olsen's crush on her, Melanie thought. And if one didn't work, she'd try them all.

She was still deciding which one to try first when her mother called to her that it was time for the teen taxi to leave. "We have to go a little early to give Brian time to load his bricks and boards," said her mother when she got to the kitchen.

"Right," grumbled Melanie.

"And, sweetheart," her mother added, handing her a stack of papers, "here are some flyers about the teen taxi. Would you take them to school and put them around in places where a lot of kids will see them? I'd really appreciate it. I simply have to get more riders."

Melanie took the flyers without responding. How could her mother ask her to do such a thing? She would have to think of some way to get rid of them. Would her mother believe her if she said she lost them?

She stuck a bran muffin into the microwave for thirty seconds, wrapped it in a paper napkin, and followed her mother and Jeffy to the van. She would need all the energy the muffin could give her to face Brian Olsen and put her plan to work.

Brian was waiting at the end of his driveway when the van pulled up, and beside him in a cardboard box were at least fifteen bricks. A couple of boards stuck out the top. Melanie sighed and closed her eyes. Why? she thought. Why, oh, why did this happen to me? Why do I have to be the one who shows up at school with The Incredible Hulk and his load of bricks?

When she opened her eyes again, Brian had put the bricks inside the van and had gone back for his books with Jeffy trotting along beside him. "Hi, Melanie," Brian called out when he stepped back inside and closed the door. "Today's the big day, and I'm ready. Sit in the front row at the assembly, and I'll wave to you."

"Thanks, Brian. I'll do my best," Melanie said, trying unsuccessfully to sound sincere. Deep down she knew she would sit as far back in the auditorium as she possibly could and probably cover her face with her sweater.

"I want to go to the 'sembly," cried Jeffy. "I want to go!"

"Well, you can't," Melanie said crossly as she tried to corral him to put him into his seat. "It's just for big kids."

"Come back here and sit with me, Jeffy," said Brian. "I'll buckle you into your seat and then let you feel my muscles."

"Can I, Mom? Can I?" Jeffy shouted.

Mrs. Edwards gave her approval, and Jeffy slid onto the bench seat at the back of the van with Brian, glowing with admiration. As he promised he would, Brian buckled Jeffy in and then held out an arm, flexing his biceps and grinning proudly.

"Oh, brother," whispered Melanie. She tried to scoot down in her seat and hoped Brian would forget she was there.

"Hey, Melanie. What do you think of this?" Brian called out.

Without meaning to, Melanie turned and looked. Brian was holding his right arm in an L-shaped position and rippling his muscles so that it looked as if giant kernels of popcorn were exploding under his shirt.

Melanie smiled weakly, but her mind was racing. Now was the perfect time to try one of the turnoffs she and her friends had gotten from the boys. But which one? Superior attitude? No, right now Brian was the one with the superior attitude. Talk about other guys? Who could she possibly bring up with muscles as big as Brian's? Say nasty things about other girls? She would have to give more thought to that one. Renege on a promise? What had she promised him? Point out his bad habits? Eeek! Everything he did was a bad habit. Talk about her diet? Not with her mother listening in. Be insincere? She had already done that by saying she'd sit in the front row during the assembly.

Desperately Melanie started through the list again. Surely there was one that would apply to the situation she was in at the moment. But which one? While she was thinking, her mother pulled the van into the unloading zone in front of Wakeman Junior High, and Brian got out, calling to some of his friends to help him unload his bricks.

Melanie glanced out the window as she gathered up her books and prepared to leave the van. She couldn't be sure, but it looked as if there were several more kids standing around the unloading area than there had been the day before, and it also looked as if they were watching the activity at the teen taxi.

They're here to watch Brian Olsen make a spectacle of himself, she thought angrily.

"I'll see you after school," her mother called out in a cheery voice.

Melanie said good-bye and jumped out of the van and headed for the building, hoping that her mother would drive away without noticing that she had left the flyers on the floor of the van. She would deal with those tomorrow. Today she had enough problems with Brian Olsen.

She tried to duck through the crowd, but she stopped cold when a girl's voice rang out, "From what I hear, things are pretty lovey in the backseat of that van."

Melanie's heart was pounding as she whirled around and scanned the groups of kids, but she couldn't figure out who had said it. The voice had not sounded familiar, and all the girls standing around looked perfectly innocent. *It's a lie!* she wanted to shout, but just as she opened her mouth to say it, she caught sight of Garrett Boldt. He was standing only a few feet away, so she knew he had heard, and he was looking at her with a puzzled expression on his face.

Oh, no, she thought. He *believes* it! But before she could decide what to do, he turned and walked away.

CHAPTER

11

*N*ow what am I going to do? Melanie asked herself over and over again through her morning classes. Not only did Garrett Boldt believe that something was going on between herself and Brian Olsen in the backseat of the van, but if she canceled out on assisting him when he photographed the drama club rehearsal after school, he would think she was reneging on a promise.

"I'm *doomed*," she moaned to her friends as they filed into the auditorium for assembly later after lunch.

Katie shook her head. "Why is it that your problems always have something to do with boys?"

"Because boys are important," huffed Melanie.

"Besides, how would *you* feel if everyone thought you liked Brian Olsen?"

"I thought you were going to use all the turnoffs we got from our boyfriends to get him to stop bugging you," said Beth.

"I am," said Melanie. "I just have to figure out how."

They found seats near the back of the room, and Melanie was just getting settled when Sara Sawyer, who was sitting in the row in front of her, turned around and said, "Melanie Edwards. Is it true what I've been hearing about you and Brian Olsen?"

Melanie's eyes bugged out and she scrunched down in her seat, trying to be less noticeable. "What did you hear?" she whispered hoarsely.

"Just that Brian is telling everybody that since he's the only rider in the teen taxi, the two of you have gotten really well acquainted. He's making it sound as if *something's going on*—if you know what I mean."

"Of course I know what you mean!" Melanie said angrily. "And it isn't true! And you can tell everybody that I said so!"

Sara shrugged. "Sure," she said, and then she giggled and turned around.

Melanie could feel tears stinging her eyes and anger welling up inside her like a volcano ready to blow. She was reaching forward to tap Sara on the shoulder and give her a large piece of her mind when

Mr. Bell walked out on the stage to begin the assembly.

"Boys and girls," he began, "today we are privileged to have a very special program. We are going to see a karate demonstration put on by ten students of Mr. Hayashida's School of Karate, who also happen to be students right here at Wakeman Junior High."

Mr. Bell paused and there was thunderous applause. Melanie clapped, too, thinking that most kids would applaud for anything that would get them out of class. She glanced at her watch, wondering how long the assembly would last and if Brian would do something weird to embarrass her in front of the whole school.

A tall, thin Asian man walked to the center of the stage, where a large mat had been placed, and introduced himself as Mr. Hayashida. He bowed respectfully to Mr. Bell and then gestured to direct the audience's attention to ten teenagers, all wearing the traditional white pants and shirts with belts ranging in color from yellow to brown, who were filing onto the stage. Melanie recognized all of them, although she only knew three by name. Brian wore a brown belt. He was the biggest and also the last one in the line, which stopped behind the mat and then bowed to Mr. Hayashida.

Melanie drew in a deep breath and crossed her

fingers for luck. Then she looked at her watch again. Only two minutes had passed. She half-listened as Mr. Hayashida explained that *karate* was a Japanese word meaning "the empty hand" and that the reason it was called that was that people who practice karate face the world without any kind of weapon except for their disciplined minds and their skill. Then he announced that it was time for the demonstration to begin.

Two boys and a girl came forward and showed the basic exercises that prepared the students for more advanced moves. Next came a demonstration on punching techniques, followed by four students who did incredible kicks. Each time, the students bowed to Mr. Hayashida and then to the audience before they began, and then they bowed again when they were finished. While they were going through their routines, Melanie's eyes roamed around the auditorium. She was too nervous about Brian's performance to be able to watch the others. What if he wanted her to come up on the stage with him? What if he asked where she was sitting? She'd be so embarrassed that she'd probably die.

Finally the moment came that she had been dreading. Mr. Hayashida bowed to the audience and said, "Now for the most important moment of our demonstration. You will see an incredible feat of discipline and skill. Brian Olsen, an advanced brown belt, will demonstrate *tameshiwara*, the ancient art of breaking objects with his bare hands."

A ripple of surprise went through the audience, and Melanie ducked lower in her seat. Next to her, Christie gave her a sympathetic look and then reached across and squeezed her hand.

The crowd got quiet as Brian stepped forward and made his bows. Then he carefully brought the bricks onstage and placed them in two waist-high columns in front of him. Next he placed two boards across the top. Melanie held her breath. So far he wasn't doing anything the least bit weird. In fact, she had never seen such a look of concentration on his face. He stepped back, holding his arm outstretched with the side of his hand above the boards like the cutting edge of a knife.

Suddenly he let out a bloodcurdling yell. "*ELAAA-NEEE!*" Then he lunged toward the boards, bringing the side of his hand down on them in a gigantic chop that broke them straight down the middle.

"Wow," she whispered, but the sound was lost in deafening applause.

"Did you see that?" Beth asked, jabbing her in the ribs with an elbow.

Mr. Hayashida held up his hand for silence as Brian prepared for his next feat. This time he went to the side of the stage and returned with another brick, which he placed across the top of the two columns where the boards had been. Then he bowed again and assumed the same position as before.

"He can't really do that," Katie whispered. "It has to be an optical illusion."

"*ELAAA-NEEE!*" he yelled again as his hand came crashing down on the brick, splintering it into a thousand pieces.

The crowd went crazy as Brian bowed to everybody and the demonstration ended. Melanie left the auditorium with the others, feeling totally confused. She had seen *The Karate Kid*, and she knew how much hard work and discipline it took to become good. So why was it that Brian could do something so special some of the time and yet he acted like a total moron the rest of the time?

Maybe I'm being too hard on him, she thought. Maybe I should give him more of a chance. Just then she heard a commotion in the hallway behind her. Turning, she saw the crowd parting and Brian Olsen rushing forward. He was out of breath, but he was coming straight toward her with a big grin on his face.

"Brian, what is it?" she demanded.

"Here," he said, thrusting something into her hand. "It's for you. I want you to have it."

Several kids had stopped to see what was going on, and he stood there, panting heavily and waiting

for her response. Melanie frowned. What was he
talking about? What did he want her to have? Looking down, she opened her hand.

"A piece of brick?" she shrieked.

"That's right," Brian said proudly. "That was
really your name that I was shouting when I was up
there on the stage, and I broke it just for you."

CHAPTER

12

*M*elanie sat in her next class trying to get the ring of laughter out of her ears. She had been absolutely mortified that everyone who had stopped in the hall to hear Brian give her the piece of brick had broken up laughing, and she had muttered a fast "Thank you" to Brian and gotten out of there as quickly as she could.

Now, sitting in Family Living class, she knew that there was no way in the world that she could ride home with him in the van today. How could she possibly face someone who had yelled her name when he smashed a brick with his bare hands in front of the entire school and then said he did it for her?

Besides, she was determined to go along with Garrett when he photographed the rehearsal of the drama club.

But how could she get out of riding home in the van? She played the upcoming scene in her mind and saw herself hovering over Jeffy to keep from having to talk to Brian. *Jeffy!* Why hadn't she thought of him before? He just might be her out.

When Family Living class ended, she raced through the crowded halls to the school office and slid to a stop beside Miss Simone's desk.

"Could I use the phone? Please?" she begged. "I have to call my mother. It's an emergency."

Miss Simone looked up from her electric typewriter and regarded Melanie solemnly. "An emergency?" she said in a calm voice. "Perhaps I can help you? Do you need to see the nurse?"

"Oh, no," Melanie assured her. "It's nothing like that. It's just that my mom is expecting me to ride home with her after school, and, well . . . something's come up . . ." Her voice trailed off as she realized that what she was saying wouldn't sound like much of an emergency to Miss Simone. "It's really important. Honest," she added, putting as much sincerity into her voice as she could.

Miss Simone sighed as if to say that she had heard the same story a million times before and pointed to the telephone on the attendance desk. "You can use that one over there," she said. "And please keep your conversation short."

Melanie thanked her and dialed her own number, cupping her hand around the mouthpiece when her mother answered.

"Mom," she said just above a whisper so that Miss Simone wouldn't be able to hear. "This is Melanie."

"Yes, dear. Is something wrong?"

Melanie could hear alarm in her mother's voice so she quickly assured her that everything was okay. "I just need to stay after school this afternoon to work on something. I'll explain later. It's really important, and I wanted to ask you if it's okay."

"Melanie. You know that I need you to help me with Jeffy while we have a passenger in the van," her mother said sharply. "We've been through this all before. Of course you can't stay after school today."

Melanie took a deep breath. She had been prepared for her mother to say that. "But Mom. You don't need me to take care of Jeffy. He always sits with Brian, and Brian makes sure he has his seat belt fastened and entertains him for the entire trip. I'm just in the way." Melanie winced when she realized what she had just said. Saying that she was just in the way was taking things a bit too far.

"You are not *just in the way*, young lady," her mother replied. "And I don't want you to get started making excuses for not riding in the teen taxi. It's a very bad habit to get into when you know that I'm depending on you for help. I want you to be on the curb when the van pulls up today. Do you understand?"

"Yes, Mom," Melanie mumbled, and hung up the phone. There was no use arguing any longer. Her mother would never give in.

When the bell rang dismissing classes for the day, Melanie hurried to the yearbook room. She knew her mother would be angry if she was late showing up for the teen taxi, but she had to explain to Garrett that she wouldn't be able to help him today.

Garrett was already there, and as usual, he was fumbling with his camera, his tripod, and all his books.

Coming up beside him, she took a deep breath and started talking before she could lose her nerve. "I'm awfully sorry, Garrett, but I won't be able to be your assistant today. I'm not reneging on my promise. It's just that my mom says that I have to ride along and take care of my little brother while she's driving the teen taxi."

"What?" asked Garrett, screwing up his face in disbelief. "You *have* to ride along?"

Melanie nodded. "It's true. Jeffy can be a little monster sometimes."

"Is Jeffy the reason you're riding in the van, or

Brian?" Garrett challenged. Then he hiked the camera strap up on his shoulder, turned, and walked away, leaving Melanie staring after him.

"But Garrett . . ." she whispered. She wanted to run after him and explain some more, but her chin was quivering so hard that she wasn't sure if she could talk. He *did* think that she was reneging on her promise. But worse than that, he actually believed that she liked Brian Olsen.

CHAPTER

13

*M*elanie was furious as she stomped out of the building and made her way across the school ground toward the teen taxi. Why hadn't her mother let her stay to help Garrett? Then she wouldn't be in this predicament. In fact, everything was her mother's fault, her mother's and the teen taxi's. Some career. It was ruining Melanie's life. There was no way that she could stop her mother from driving the taxi, but she could get Brian Olsen to leave her alone.

As she approached the van, she was surprised to see Brian already inside with Jeffy on his lap. She had half-expected to see him demonstrating karate kicks on the sidewalk.

"Hi, Melanie," called out Jeffy. "Big Brian is

showing me the callouses on his hands. He has to have them to protect his hands when he breaks bricks," Jeffy said, obviously proud of his knowledge.

Melanie nodded to Jeffy, but she barely looked at Brian as she sat down. There was one thing she could do, she decided. She would throw everything at him that the boys had said they didn't like about girls. If that didn't do the trick, then she was definitely doomed.

She opened her notebook and peeked at the page where she had written the turnoffs. "Okay," she whispered under her breath. "Here goes."

Just before the taxi pulled away from the curb she moved back in the van to the seat directly in front of Brian. She would have to be careful that her mother didn't hear what she was about to say and come totally unglued at her for acting obnoxious. Of course her mother didn't know what an embarrassment Brian had become for her, she reasoned. And she wouldn't understand even if Melanie told her.

Pasting a fake smile on her face, she asked in a voice too soft for her mother to hear, "Brian, did you know that Laura McCall forces her friends to do special favors for her or they can't be her friends anymore?" It was the nastiest thing she could think of to say about any girl in Wakeman Junior High, and besides, it was true.

Brian looked puzzled. "No," he said, shaking his head. "Where did you hear a rumor like that?"

"Oh, everybody knows about it. At least, all the girls do," she said.

Brian frowned slightly and went back to talking to Jeffy. Okay for number one, she thought, and peeked at her list again. Number two was "superior attitude." That would be easy.

Melanie glanced at her mother again, but Mrs. Edwards's attention was on traffic, and she seemed oblivious to the conversation in the back of the van. "Of course *I* would never treat my friends so badly," she went on. "*I* happen to care about my friends. Actually, *I* care about a lot of things. The homeless. The environment. The war against drugs. *I* absolutely can't stand people who aren't caring."

This time when Brian looked up, he shrugged and gave her an embarrassed grin.

Melanie was beginning to feel exuberant. It was working. Brian certainly wasn't giving her his dopey, lovesick grin now. "Or who are insincere," she added. "I absolutely can't stand people who say they care about something and then never do anything about it. I plan to do something about the homeless, the environment, and the war against drugs just as soon as I have time," she said, trying her best to sound totally insincere.

By now Brian was squirming uncomfortably, and

Melanie could hardly keep from giggling out loud. She took a deep breath and thought about what to say next. She would skip talking about her diet and about reneging on promises for the time being. They would take some planning. Instead she would go on to talking about other guys and to pointing out Brian's faults and bad habits.

But which other boys would she talk about? A lump jumped into her throat at the thought of Garrett. She couldn't possibly talk about him. Not after what had just happened. And what about Shane and Scott? She really liked both of them, and she would feel strange talking about them in a situation like this. Before she had time to decide, her mother swung the van into Brian's driveway.

"You kids will have to finish your conversation in the morning," Mrs. Edwards sang out happily. "Here you are, Brian. Home safe and sound."

Brian said good-bye to Jeffy, thanked Mrs. Edwards, and ducked out of the van without a word to Melanie. Gleefully she watched him slide the box containing the leftover bricks off the floor and close the taxi door behind himself, thinking that she would definitely finish the conversation in the morning. If Mom only knew, Melanie thought. In the meantime, she had come up with another idea.

She made a beeline for the phone as soon as she

got home and dialed Shawnie Pendergast's number. Shawnie answered.

"Hi, this is Melanie Edwards," she began. Then she looked around the kitchen to be sure her mother was out of hearing range. "Do you remember the other day when we were talking about the teen taxi, and I said that my mother was a rotten driver?"

"Sure," Shawnie replied. "That made me nervous, and when I told my parents, they said I shouldn't ride with her."

"That's what I thought," said Melanie. "Well, I have a confession to make. I was only joking. My mom's really a great driver, and maybe your parents should reconsider letting you ride with her."

Shawnie sounded a little surprised, but she promised to talk to her parents as soon as they got home, and Melanie scanned the phone book looking for Kevin Walker-Noles's and Michelle Troyer's numbers, thinking that if she could get a few more kids to ride in her mother's teen taxi, then even if Brian Olsen continued to have a crush on her, he wouldn't be able to say that anything romantic was going on between them in the backseat. She would have *witnesses*!

When she talked to Kevin, he said that he had noticed how the taxi had been on time to school every day so far and that he definitely wanted to ride. Before they hung up, he said that he would ask his parents to talk to Mrs. Edwards.

As usual, Michelle didn't have much to say when Melanie confessed that the taxi wasn't as crowded as she had said it would be, so Melanie didn't really know if she would sign up again or not.

Melanie was feeling a hundred times better when she finished the calls. She would talk to some other kids at school tomorrow and she would get the flyers off the van floor and tape them on bulletin boards and even on the mirror in the girls' bathroom. With any luck at all, she would have the van filled in no time. She chuckled as she remembered how she had done everything she could think of to keep her mother from starting the teen taxi in the first place, and now, here she was trying her best to get riders so that she wouldn't have to be alone with Brian Olsen.

She picked up her books and was heading for her room when she passed the front door. At that instant the doorbell rang. Melanie set her books on the bottom stair and opened the door. A tall man wearing a suit and tie stood there, holding the hand of a little boy about Jeffy's age. Maybe he's come to play with Jeffy, Melanie thought.

"Hi," she said to the man. "Can I help you?"

"Yes, I think you can," he said pleasantly. "I'm Mr. Dotson and this is my son, Jeremy. We've come about the puppies."

Puppies! Melanie stared first at the man and then at the little boy. She had forgotten all about the ad to give away the puppies.

"This is the right house, isn't it?" the man asked apprehensively.

Melanie's first impulse was to say no and slam the door, but she heard her mother in the foyer behind her.

"Who is it, dear? Is it someone about the puppies?"

Nodding silently, Melanie opened the door wider, and the man and the little boy stepped inside.

CHAPTER

14

"Garrett!" Melanie shrieked. "You let them take Garrett!"

She had stayed in her room while Mr. Dotson and his son had been there and had only come back downstairs when she heard the front door slam and a car start up at the front curb. Now she stood at the bottom of the basement steps staring into the box where Rainbow sat, calmly licking one of only seven remaining puppies. She had been so happy to see that little Katie was still there and Jana and Scott and each of the others until she realized that one puppy was missing. Multicolored like his mother, Garrett was a precious, roly-poly little dog, and now he was gone.

"What do you mean, I let them take Garrett?" her

mother asked. "Did you name the puppies after we told you specifically that you weren't to do that? Oh, Melanie," her mother said with a sigh. She looked suddenly sympathetic and put an arm around Melanie's shoulder. "We tried to explain that if you gave the puppies names, then they would take on personalities, too, and it would be twice as difficult to say good-bye to them when the time came to give them away."

Melanie dropped to her knees beside the box. "Well, I couldn't help it," she sobbed. "I couldn't just call them Dog One or Dog Two. Besides, they already had personalities. And they were all my super good friends, just like the friends they were named after."

Her mother sighed. "Maybe you'd better tell me the rest of their names," she said.

Reaching into the box, Melanie pulled out a curly brown pup. "This is Beth," she said, putting the dog down again beside Rainbow. "And this is Jana." This time she held up a brown and white baby. Setting her back in the box, she raised the little red puppy for her mother to see.

"Don't tell me. Let me guess," said Mrs. Edwards. "That's Katie."

"Right," said Melanie. Then she pointed out Christie, Shane, Scott, and Jason.

"Jason?" her mother asked with a frown.

"He's somebody new," Melanie added hastily. She didn't dare admit that he was the television star on the life-size poster in her room. Not now, just when her mother was starting to act a little bit sympathetic. "And what about Rainbow?" she went on. "She'll be brokenhearted if we give away all of her children."

Mrs. Edwards knelt beside the box and slowly stroked Rainbow on the head. The mother dog raised her eyes and seemed to smile. "You know, honey," her mother began in a soft voice. "Someday you and Jeffy are going to grow up and leave home. You'll go off to college or get a job or get married or maybe all three. And your father and I will be sad in some ways, and we'll definitely miss you, but we'll know that it's how things are supposed to be."

She paused, and Melanie felt tears well up in her eyes. She knew what her mother was getting at, but she didn't want to hear it.

"It's the same for Rainbow and her puppies," Mrs. Edwards went on. "They're going to go off into the world and make a lot of other families happy just the same way Rainbow has made us happy. Now we can be sad about that, but we have to let it happen, don't we?"

Melanie couldn't answer. The tears were flowing too hard. She couldn't stand to think of all eight puppies being taken away.

"But what if the people who take them are mean to them?" she blubbered. "Oh, Mom. What if they beat them or starve them or something?"

"Things like that do happen," her mother admitted. "So we'll just have to be very careful and look over each person who wants a puppy. I don't think that Mr. Dotson and his little boy, Jeremy, looked as if they would be mean to Garrett, do you?"

Melanie sniffed loudly and shook her head.

"In fact," said her mother, "I'll bet that right this very minute he's the center of attention in their house."

"I'll bet he even gets to *sleep* with Jeremy!" shouted Jeffy.

Startled, Melanie turned to see that Jeffy had come down the stairs and was standing behind her with a big grin on his face. Then his face clouded and he added, "I hope he doesn't pee in Jeremy's bed."

"Oh, Jeffy. You just don't understand," Melanie blurted as she pushed past him and hurried to her room, where she planned to stay for the rest of the evening. As she flung herself onto her bed, she thought, It's so unfair. Why are so many bad things happening to me?

Mrs. Edwards was euphoric when Melanie went downstairs the next morning, which only made her own mood blacker.

"We had four more calls on the puppies last night," her mother chirped, "and two of the riders who canceled out on the teen taxi earlier have decided to give us a try after all. Isn't that great?"

Melanie nodded as she gulped down her orange juice. It *was* great. It meant that her scheme had worked and she wouldn't have to worry about Brian's spreading those ridiculous rumors anymore. Now if she could just get him to stop having a crush on her, and then if she could convince Garrett that he had been wrong about her, her life might get back to normal.

The teen taxi picked up Shawnie Pendergast first. She came bounding out of her house before the van could come to a complete stop, and when she hopped in, she practically sang out, "Hi, Mrs. Edwards. Hi, Mel. Hi, Jeffy. Gosh, this is going to be fun. I love the idea of riding to school in a teen taxi."

You've got to be kidding, Melanie thought when Shawnie sat down on the opposite side of the van and gave her a big smile. "Do you really like the idea of a teen taxi?" Melanie asked in disbelief.

"Of course," Shawnie insisted. "It's better than a grungy old school bus and much nicer than a city bus that anybody can ride. It's just for teens, and that's what makes it so cool."

Cool? The word echoed in Melanie's mind. *Cool*

was the last word she would have used to describe her mother's new business.

"But wouldn't you feel weird if your mother was a taxi driver for school kids?" she asked.

"What's so weird about that?" asked Shawnie in surprise.

Melanie didn't answer because the van was pulling into Kevin's driveway. Kevin raced out of his house and hurried toward the taxi with a smile on his face.

"It's great to have my own personal limo service," he said as he clambered aboard.

Good grief, thought Melanie. Kevin thinks the teen taxi is cool, too.

When they stopped at Brian's house, Melanie smiled to herself. Things were working out better than she had hoped. She had been trying to figure out how to talk about other great boys to Brian, but how did you talk to one boy about other guys without letting your embarrassment show? But now she knew. The idea had just come to her, and it was going to work like a charm.

Brian lumbered into the van with his head down, but his eyes lit up and a smile spread across his face when he saw the two new riders. "Hey, Kev! Hey, Shawnie! All right!" he said, slapping hands with Kevin. "When did you guys sign on?"

Kevin and Shawnie began talking at once, explaining to Brian that their parents had decided to let them ride the taxi and had called Mrs. Edwards the night before. Melanie listened patiently, waiting for a break in the conversation and the familiar adoring look from Brian to begin her plan.

But Brian didn't look at her. Instead, he lifted Jeffy onto his lap and kept right on talking to Kevin and Shawnie as if she weren't there.

The van moved out of the residential neighborhood and into the heavier traffic on the route to Wakeman Junior High. Melanie bit her lower lip and looked out the window, wondering what had come over Brian. He hadn't even said hello to her, much less acted like a lovesick moose, the way he usually did. Finally she couldn't stand it any longer.

Turning toward the others, she said, "Shawnie. Don't you think that Scott Daly is one of the best-looking hunks in Wacko? I mean, he is a living doll. Don't you agree?"

Shawnie darted quick glances at both Kevin and Brian before she answered. "Sure. He's really cute. What made you ask?"

Melanie could see out of the corner of her eye that she had Brian's attention. That was exactly what she wanted. Curtis Trowbridge had said it really made him mad for girls to talk about how great other guys were. With Shawnie's help, maybe it would have the same effect on Brian.

"What made me ask?" Melanie echoed Shawnie's question. "Oh, I don't know. I guess I was just thinking about great guys, and naturally Scott popped into my mind. At least he's not like some guys I know," she went on, unable to stop now that she had gotten started talking. "You know, the show-offs. The ones who are always *demonstrating* how strong they are and things like that."

"Brian is not a show-off!" cried Jeffy. He wriggled out of Brian's lap and stumbled toward Melanie, grabbing the arm of her chair for support. "He's my *friend*!"

Melanie was stunned. Everyone was looking at her. "I . . . I wasn't talking about Brian," she murmured, but she knew they could all tell that she was lying. She wanted to tell Brian that she hadn't meant to hurt his feelings, but she couldn't even turn her head toward him, much less look him in the eye.

Finally the van stopped in front of the school. Brian got out without a word. Kevin followed. Shawnie seemed to want to say something to Melanie, but after a minute she shrugged and got out, too. Finally Melanie stepped out and trudged across the grass, shaking her head. What have I done? she asked herself.

CHAPTER

15

"Flash! Big news!" called out Beth, who came sliding across the cafeteria floor toward the table where the rest of The Fabulous Five were sitting. She had a lunch bag in one hand and was balancing a carton of chocolate milk on her head.

"What kind of big news?" Melanie asked anxiously. Her mood had improved since the van ride earlier in the morning, but she was still a little jumpy.

"Brian is telling stories about you again, but this time they're not about making out in the back of the van," said Beth.

"What!" cried Melanie. "What's he saying?"

"Are you ready for this?" insisted Beth. Then she

tipped her head sideways and let the carton of milk drop into her hand.

Melanie nodded.

"Okay. Here goes. He's saying that you aren't the kind of girl that he thought you were, that you're snotty and conceited and a big gossip, and that he doesn't like you anymore."

Melanie sucked in her breath. "Oh, my gosh. Who told you that?"

"Keith," Beth answered. "He heard him say it in English class. Keith also said that it really surprised him because Brian usually talks nonstop about how great you are. He asked me if I knew why Brian changed his mind about you, and of course, I said no."

"Why the long face, Mel?" cried Katie. "That's exactly what you wanted Brian to think, isn't it?"

Melanie felt a lump forming in her throat. "I thought it was," she said slowly. "But now I'm not so sure. I mean, you should have been there yesterday on the way home and again this morning. Especially this morning. I really said some terrible things, and Brian knew some of them were about him. Even Jeffy knew. I feel like a total jerk. I didn't mean to hurt him. I just wanted him to leave me alone."

"Do you really think you hurt him?" asked Jana. "Maybe he's just mad."

"No, he's hurt," said Melanie. "He wouldn't even look at me when he got out of the van. I don't blame him for thinking I'm a terrible person. I deserve it. I just wish he wasn't spreading it around the entire school."

"But people who really know you understand that you're not that way," Christie reassured her.

"Right," said Jana. "You're one of the *nicest* people in the world. That's why we're best friends."

"Tell that to Brian Olsen," Melanie said sourly. "Besides, you know how kids love gossip. Lots of them will believe it, no matter what they thought of me before. I just hope Laura McCall and her Fantastic Foursome friends don't hear about it. If they do, they'll make posters and tape them all over school."

Melanie picked up her sandwich crusts and apple core and stuffed them back in her lunch bag. "That reminds me," she said. "I promised my mom that I'd put up some flyers about the teen taxi, and I was too upset to do it this morning. I'll see you guys later."

"If you want to wait a couple of minutes until the rest of us are finished, we'll go with you," offered Christie.

"That's okay," said Melanie. "I'll go ahead and meet you outside in a few minutes."

She tossed her lunch trash into the garbage can by the cafeteria door and headed toward the girls' bathroom where she planned to tape one of the flyers to the mirror. Every girl in school would be sure to see it there, she thought, and chuckled to herself in spite of her problems. When she had finished, she stood back and took a good look at the flyer for the first time.

Stuck Without a Ride to School?
Catch Edwards's Teen Taxi and Join Your
Friends
Private Van Service Door-to-door
Call 555-4009

Melanie sighed, thinking how hard her mother was trying to make her new business work. Not only that, but the only ones at school who had teased her about the taxi or made fun of her mother for being a taxi driver were Laura McCall and her friends from The Fantastic Foursome. That was to be expected since they never passed up an opportunity to start trouble between the rival cliques. Actually, the teen taxi hadn't been an embarrassment at all. Shawnie and Kevin had both been glad to ride, and of course Brian . . .

Her thought trailed off as she tried to put Brian out of her mind and concentrate on helping her mother. She knew down deep that she ought to do more than just put up flyers and hope for the best.

Turning to leave, she stopped and went back to the mirror and pulled a ballpoint pen out of her purse. Underneath the phone number she added:

Or See Melanie Edwards at School

Leaving the girls' room, she hurried down the hall toward the big bulletin board beside the office. Most kids checked it every day or so because any new events going on at school were posted there.

Just about everybody was still in the cafeteria eating lunch, and Melanie's footsteps echoed in the deserted hallway. She scanned the crowded bulletin board, looking for a place to put the flyer among notices about school club events, swim team tryouts at the YMCA, and a variety of other things. There's so much junk up there, she thought, that nobody will see mine unless I rearrange things. She began clearing a space in the lower left-hand corner, which was the spot nearest the drinking fountain and where a lot of students would be likely to see it. She was so intent on her task that she was barely aware of someone else's footsteps coming closer and closer until they were almost there. Then they stopped.

Startled, she looked up into Brian Olsen's face and felt her own face turn red. He looked equally startled, and then he looked down and coughed a fake-sounding cough.

Oh, no, she thought. He's embarrassed, too. Now what am I going to do? Words filled her mind. *Sorry. Didn't mean it the way it sounded. Don't think I'm awful. Sorry. Sorry. Sorry.* But her tongue was frozen and nothing came out.

What was probably only seconds seemed like an hour as they stood there facing each other. Finally, Brian murmured, "Hi, Mel," and walked on by, leaving her staring at a spot on the floor and feeling as if her heart would burst.

CHAPTER

16

*B*rian was quiet again on the ride home, and Melanie's depression deepened. She knew that she should try to fix things between them. She should apologize. Or if she couldn't do that, she should ask someone else to give him the message that she was sorry for acting like a jerk. But what if she did and he started liking her again? Her mind reeled at the thought of more brick-smashing demonstrations where he yelled out her name, or of him chinning himself for her again in front of the entire student body. Or worst of all, of anyone's thinking that she liked him back. As badly as she wanted to make things right, she didn't want that to happen.

Maybe if I just ignore the whole situation, it will

go away, she told herself. Maybe he'll forget all about me. Maybe he'll even get interested in somebody else. But one look at the forlorn expression on Brian's face told her that he wouldn't. Not very soon, anyway.

For the next few days, Melanie had a lot of other things to occupy her mind. Two eighth-graders and a ninth-grader signed on for the teen taxi. Counting herself, that made seven junior-high passengers, which was the limit the van could hold, and except for the tension between her and Brian, trips to and from school took on a party atmosphere. Her mother was ecstatic, and Jeffy was running around the house shouting about all his new friends, and Melanie was miserable.

More of the puppies went to new homes, also. Scott was taken by an elderly friend of their neighbor's, Mrs. Miller, and Melanie consoled herself that the old gentleman was lonely and that Scott would be a good friend to him. Christie was chosen by Jeffy's kindergarten teacher, Ms. Strickland, who promised they could visit her anytime they wanted. But the hardest time came one afternoon when Melanie came home from riding her bike to Jana's and her mother met her at the door.

"There is a family downstairs with the puppies," she said, "and I think they're going to take Katie."

A lump the size of a tennis ball filled Melanie's

throat. "Katie?" she whispered in disbelief. Red-haired Katie had become Melanie's favorite, and she had laughed and told herself so many times that the little dog's personality was identical to Katie Shannon's. Little Katie was always in the middle of everything, growling at the boy dogs and making sure that she got her fair share of the puppy food.

"Why don't you go down and meet them?" her mother said gently.

Melanie took a deep breath and willed the tears not to fill her eyes. Of course she wanted to meet them. She couldn't send Katie home with just anyone. She counted off the steps as she went down, not wanting to look at the man and woman and small girl about Jeffy's age who stood beside Rainbow's box.

"Hello," said the woman when Melanie approached. "I'm Mrs. Hayward. This is my husband and my daughter, Janelle."

Melanie cleared her throat and said in a shaky voice, "Hi, I'm Melanie Edwards."

She glanced at Janelle, who was cradling Katie on her shoulder, but the little girl's face was solemn and her eyes were brimming with tears. Melanie frowned. If she wanted a puppy, why wasn't she smiling? Maybe she didn't even like dogs and would be mean to little Katie.

"Janelle's feeling sad," Mrs. Hayward explained. "Last week Maxie was hit by a car and killed. Maxie was Janelle's best friend. We got him as a puppy when she was just a baby so they had been together forever."

Melanie looked back at the sad little girl as sympathy filled her heart. "Oh . . . I'm sorry," she almost whispered. Then she took a deep breath and knelt beside Janelle, stroking Katie's curly red head. "I call her Katie," she said, "because she reminds me so much of one of my best friends, Katie Shannon. She loves to play, especially tug-of-war."

Just then Katie stuck out her tiny pink tongue and licked Janelle squarely on the nose as if to say she liked the little girl. Janelle's face lit up and she planted a kiss on top of Katie's head and pressed her cheek against the little dog's head. Melanie smiled in spite of the ache in her heart. Katie was going to have a good home. *She was going to be loved.*

Melanie didn't have to worry about talking to Brian on the way to or from school now. With the teen taxi so full, she always had someone else to talk to. Not only that, Jeffy was the center of attention, hopping from one teenager to another and loving every minute of it. It was almost impossible to get him to sit still and buckle up except when he sat with Brian and admired his muscular arms and chest. Jeffy liked everybody, especially the girls.

"I think he's learning to flirt," said Holly Davis,

one of the new riders. "Look at the way he rolls his eyes and grins."

It was true, thought Melanie. Jeffy was so busy showing off and clowning for the others that she barely had to deal with him at all, and her mother didn't seem to mind that he sat with first one and then another of the riders as long as he buckled up.

One afternoon after they had delivered all their passengers and were home again, her mother looked thoughtful and then said, "Mel, do you remember when we were starting up the taxi and I needed your help and that I told you eventually we'd work things out so that you wouldn't have to give up your social life?"

Melanie nodded. What was her mother getting at? she wondered.

"Well, I've decided that Jeffy is so well taken care of by the boys and girls who ride with me that it isn't necessary for you to come along anymore, if you don't want to. I appreciate all the help you've given me, but now you're free to go to Bumpers with The Fabulous Five or help your friend Garrett out with his photography assignments or do whatever you wish."

Melanie's mouth dropped open, and she stared at her mother, who looked back at her with genuine appreciation shining on her face.

"Gosh . . . thanks . . . I mean," Melanie sputtered.

"Without you, I never could have gotten my business going," Mrs. Edwards said proudly. "And I'm the one who's doing the thanking. You don't know how much making the teen taxi service work has meant to me."

Melanie saw tears fill her mother's eyes, and the guilt that she had tried to push out of her mind while she was sabotaging the teen taxi came rushing back in.

"Mom," she said softly. "There's something you ought to know. It's my fault that Shawnie and Kevin canceled. I told Shawnie that you were a bad driver and Kevin that you were always running late. It's my fault that Michelle canceled, too. She's awfully shy, especially around boys, so I told her that . . ." Melanie cleared her throat, wishing there was something else to say. Sighing, she said, "I told her she'd have to sit on a boy's lap because the van was so crowded."

"What?" gasped her mother. "Melanie Edwards! Why on earth did you do a thing like that?"

Melanie closed her eyes. She had to tell her mother the truth. There was no other way. "I was embarrassed about the teen taxi. I was afraid kids would tease me and make fun of you, saying my mother was a taxi driver."

"Oh, I see." Mrs. Edwards frowned to herself. Then she looked at Melanie with concern and asked, "And did they?"

Melanie shook her head. "I guess I was worried

for nothing," she confessed. "And Shawnie even said she thought the teen taxi was *cool*."

Her mother chuckled and put her arm around Melanie's shoulder. "I guess everything worked out all right then, didn't it?"

Melanie tried to smile, but she couldn't. "Not quite," she said. "There's still Brian. He had a monster crush on me and was telling everybody at school that we were making out in the back of the van."

"Oh, Melanie!" Her mother sounded shocked. "That's awful. No wonder you were upset. But Brian wouldn't do a thing like that. Someone must have told you that just to be mean. He's a darling boy, and so strong. Why, as much as you like boys, I'm surprised that you don't have a crush on *him*."

Melanie looked away quickly, crossing her eyes in exasperation. Why did parents always have such rotten taste? "Mu-*THUR*!" she groaned. "Brian Olsen's not my type. Anyway, everything's okay now. I . . . I had a talk with him."

Mrs. Edwards's face lit up. "Wonderful, sweetheart. I can always count on you to do the right thing."

Melanie cringed and her guilty feeling came back again. If only her mother knew that the talk she had had with Brian had been anything but the right thing to do. What would she think if she knew that Melanie had said everything she could to make him *not* like her anymore? She was still fumbling for words to end the conversation when the telephone rang. Grabbing the receiver, she said, "Hello. Edwardses' residence. Teen taxi service, our specialty. Melanie speaking." Her mother's smile told Melanie that she was pleased.

The caller was a man and he asked for Mrs. Edwards. Probably someone else about the puppies, she thought as she handed off the phone and escaped up the stairs to her room.

She paced the floor, too antsy to do homework. On the one hand, right after she confessed to her mother about trying to sabotage the taxi, she had turned around and stretched the truth about how she had handled Brian. But on the other hand, her prayers had been answered. Now she could get her social life back on track, and she wouldn't have to face Brian twice a day in the taxi. Maybe now she could even forget about the mess she had made of that situation. I'll call my friends, she thought, and tell them the good news.

Halfway down the stairs she met her mother coming up, and the grin on her face was bigger than ever. "Melanie, guess what?" she shouted.

"What?" Melanie asked.

"I'm going to be a celebrity," Mrs. Edwards said with a laugh. "That was the local newspaper. They're coming here in the morning to do a story about the teen taxi. They're sending a photographer, too. Isn't that exciting?"

"Gosh, Mom, that's terrific. What did they say?" asked Melanie.

"They said that they had heard about the taxi and thought it was a great idea and that I deserve recognition for providing such a badly needed service. I don't know what to think," she added with an embarrassed laugh. "I never expected anything like this."

Melanie gave her mother a hug. "They're right, you know. You do deserve recognition. Gosh, I'm really proud of you."

A little while later, after she had called her friends and given them all the good news, she telephoned Garrett.

"Hi, Garrett," she began shyly. "If you still need an assistant to help with your photography assignments, I can do it now. And I can explain all about the teen taxi."

They talked a long time, and before they hung up he said he really wanted her to help him. He even said that he'd take pictures of the teen taxi for the yearbook.

Melanie drifted back into her room and stretched out on her bed. In spite of how great everything was turning out, there was still one thing that bothered her. Brian Olsen. Why, oh, why, she asked herself, can't I get Brian out of my mind?

CHAPTER

17

The Edwards household was a madhouse the next morning with the newspaper reporter interviewing her mother and the photographer snapping pictures of the van. Jeffy was beside himself with excitement and mugged for the photographer every chance he got. Melanie watched it all with growing pride. She was sorry now that she had tried to sabotage the teen taxi, but at least everything had worked out for the best.

When the people from the newspaper finally left, she went back upstairs for her books. She paused by her desk and opened her notebook, pulling out the page where she had written the turnoffs and crumpling it into a ball, which she tossed in her wastebasket. It was no wonder that Brian hated her now.

Those were terrible things to do on purpose, and she had lain awake most of the night making up her mind about how to set things right. Crossing and uncrossing her fingers three times for luck, she hurried back down to the taxi.

When she got inside the van, she looked longingly at the seat she usually sat in. Maybe she should wait until another time to put her plan into action. She was going to Bumpers after school, but maybe she could do it tomorrow morning. No, she decided, straightening her shoulders. She wouldn't feel better until she got it over with.

She sat down on one end of the bench seat where Brian usually sat. If he would sit down beside her, they could talk on the way to school, and she could finally tell him the truth about how she felt.

As usual, Shawnie was the first passenger to be picked up, and Jeffy jumped into her lap and jabbered excitedly about the morning's events. Melanie tried to join in the conversation, but the closer they got to Brian's house the more nervous she got. Would she be able to say it right? What if he became angrier than ever?

Her heart was racing when they turned into his street, and the blood was pounding in her ears when the van pulled into his driveway. Her eyes were glued to the van door as it swung open. Brian stepped inside, closing the door behind himself, and absently headed for his usual seat. He gave her a quizzical frown when he noticed her sitting there.

Melanie turned to look at him. He was staring out the window.

"Hi, Brian," she said through quivering lips. "You don't mind if I sit with you this morning, do you?"

He seemed to think the idea over for a second and then shook his head. So far, so good, she thought, and took a deep breath to start her speech.

"Hey, Brian. Show me your muscles!" shouted Jeffy. "Can I come and sit with you?"

"Not now, Jeffy," Brian answered. "Maybe later."

They rode along in silence for a few minutes, but she knew there was no use putting it off. She had to talk to him, and she had to do it now.

"Brian, I think I owe you an apology," she began, saying the words slowly. He turned to look at her, but his expression was blank, so she couldn't guess what he was thinking.

"Actually, I *know* that I owe you an apology for acting like such a jerk and saying so many dumb things. I didn't mean to hurt your feelings."

Frowning, Brian shook his head. "I couldn't believe that was you talking. I always thought you were a great person, but then you began sounding so conceited and so . . ." Brian shrugged. "I couldn't understand what was going on. I mean, I *really* liked you before that."

"I know," Melanie said gently. "That was just the problem. Don't get me wrong. I was really flattered that you liked me so much, but the truth is I like someone else and I was trying to make you *not* like me so much. I overdid it," she said, trying to look truly sorry.

Brian didn't say anything for a minute. Finally he looked at her sadly and said, "Why didn't you just say so?"

"I don't know. Honest, I don't. But I really am sorry."

Just then the van pulled to a stop again to pick up Kevin Walker-Noles. Kevin got in, calling out a greeting to everyone inside, and Melanie held her breath. She wanted Brian to accept her apology and say he understood, but would he? If only their conversation hadn't been interrupted by the stop at Kevin's house.

Once Kevin was seated, the taxi inched out into traffic again, and Melanie glanced at Brian out of the corner of her eye. He had twisted around and was looking out the back window.

Turning back to her, he said, "I could have sworn that I heard someone honking at us. Guess I was wrong."

"Do you believe me when I say I'm sorry?" Melanie asked, getting their conversation back on track as quickly as she could.

Brian nodded. "I'm sorry, too," he said, "especially that you like someone else."

"Then, you forgive me?" she asked anxiously.

"Sure," he said, grinning broadly.

Melanie relaxed and sank down in the seat. Smiling to herself, she thought about how things had worked themselves out. Brian wasn't mad at her anymore *and* he wouldn't be doing those dumb things to show off for her in front of everyone now that he understood. Best yet, she could go to Bumpers after school with her friends and no one would tease her about Brian. *Finally*, she thought, my life is getting back to normal.

Suddenly Melanie was aware of honking, and she and Brian both turned to look out the back window at the same time.

"Hey, it's another van, and it's honking at us," she cried.

"Yeah, and it has CHANNEL 2 painted on the side," shouted Brian.

"Oh, my gosh. Mom! Pull over to the curb!" Melanie called out to her mother. "We're going to be on television!"

Mrs. Edwards eased the teen taxi out of traffic and brought it to a stop with the Channel 2 van right behind. An instant later the door flew open and Marge Whitworth, the anchorwoman from the television station, climbed inside followed by her cameraman.

"We just heard about your new taxi service. Do you mind if we ride along and tape a segment for tonight's news?" she asked.

"Of course not," chirped Mrs. Edwards. "Be my guest."

As the van started up again, Melanie leaned back and closed her eyes. Being honest with Brian had been the right thing to do. Other things were going right, too. The teen taxi was not only a success, but her mother was going to be famous. It might be starting small with the local newspaper and television appearances, but maybe next week *People* magazine would call or Johnny Carson. Who knows, she thought, maybe she'll even make *Saturday Night Live*.

Just then Brian nudged her. "Smile," he whispered.

"What?" she asked, opening her eyes and then sitting up with a start.

"I said, smile," Brian answered. "We're going to be on TV."

Melanie tried to smile, but her lips felt instantly stiff and inside she was groaning. The cameraman was pointing his Minicam directly at them, and she could see by the red light on the front that the camera was rolling. How could this be happening? Especially now, when she had just gotten Brian Olsen out of her life. They were going to be on TV, all right, sitting close together in the backseat of the van. Everyone in the world would see them. At least everyone in Wakeman Junior High.

"Oh, *no*," she muttered under her breath. "Here we go again."

CHAPTER

18

"Look at this!" Katie said, putting the teen magazine down on the table so the other members of The Fabulous Five could see what she was talking about. It was Saturday afternoon and they were sitting in Taco Plenty, the fast-food restaurant at the mall. "Can you believe that they wouldn't let the girl who wrote this letter play quarterback on a football team for nine- to twelve-year-olds? That's archaic!"

"Who wouldn't?" asked Jana.

"Why would she want to?" asked Melanie.

Katie pointed to a letter in the *Dear Bob* column. "The officials wouldn't let her, that's who. They said she could get hurt, and Bob agrees with them."

"Well, she could," agreed Beth.

"That's not the point," Katie protested. "Anyone who plays can get hurt. If she's good enough, they ought to let her do it. Girls play on baseball teams. I'm going to write *Dear Bob* and tell him what I think of him. I don't know why they let a man write this column anyway. Mostly girls read the magazine."

Christie joined in. "But football's different. It's a contact sport."

"Maybe it is, but Geena McNatt could play on a football team and do real well, if she wanted to," said Katie.

"I have to agree with you about that," said Jana, giggling. "The only reason they might not let Geena play on Wacko's team is she could hurt someone else."

"What's the big difference?" asked Melanie. "There are lots of other things she can do. Girl things."

"Don't you see?" Katie complained. "She doesn't *want* to do those other things. *That's* the big difference. That's the trouble with everybody. They say girls can do some things, but they can't do others. I don't want anyone telling me what I can or can't do."

"Well, that wouldn't happen at Wacko," said Christie. "Girls can do anything they want there."

"Hey, if you want to try out for the football team next fall, go ahead," said Beth. "I'll bet they'd let you, but I wouldn't want Geena McNatt's brother Max leaving his footprints all over me."

Katie flipped the magazine closed. "That's the trouble with everyone. They don't realize how much bias there is, even at our school. I bet Elizabeth Cady Stanton wouldn't let them get away with not letting *her* daughter play football."

Jana looked puzzled. "Who's Elizabeth Cady Stanton?" she asked.

"See!" Katie retorted. "Do any of the rest of you know who she is?" The others shook their heads.

Katie rolled her eyes. "She was only the person who started the whole women's movement, that's all. If it wasn't for her, women probably still wouldn't be able to vote."

"Look," said Beth. "When you run into something that you can't do because you're a girl, let me know. I'll help you protest. But I'm not going to get bent all out of shape over a letter to Bob."

Frustrated, Katie looked at her friends. They all seemed so unconcerned. Couldn't they recognize bias against females when they saw it?

Katie gets her chance to defend women's rights a lot sooner than she expects. Only her efforts backfire, and she finds herself in trouble with a lot of people, including Tony Calcaterra, the other girls in

Wakeman Junior High, and the school principal. But Katie also gets unexpected help from someone from a long time ago in *The Fabulous Five #19: The Boys-Only Club*.

ABOUT THE AUTHOR

Betsy Haynes, the daughter of a former news-woman, began scribbling poetry and short stories as soon as she learned to write. A serious writing career, however, had to wait until after her marriage and the arrival of her two children. But that early practice must have paid off, for within three months Mrs. Haynes had sold her first story. In addition to a number of magazine short stories and the Taffy Sinclair series, Mrs. Haynes is also the author of *The Great Mom Swap* and its sequel, *The Great Boyfriend Trap*. She lives in Colleyville, Texas, with her husband, who is also an author.

Great FREE offer just for you!

Join SNEAK PEEKS™!

Do you want to know what's new before anyone else? Do you like to read great books about girls just like you? If you do, then you won't want to miss SNEAK PEEKS™! Be the first of your friends to know what's hot ... When you join SNEAK PEEKS™, we'll send you FREE inside information in the mail about the latest books ... *before they're published!* Plus updates on your favorite series, authors, and exciting new stories filled with friendship and fun ... adventure and mystery ... girlfriends and boyfriends.

It's easy to be a member of SNEAK PEEKS™. Just fill out the coupon below ... and get ready for fun! It's FREE! Don't delay—sign up today!